**W9-BON-677**

# HOGGEE

ALSO BY ANNA MYERS

Red-Dirt Jessie

Rosie's Tiger

Graveyard Girl

Spotting the Leopard

The Keeping Room

Fire in the Hills

Ethan Between Us

Captain's Command

When the Bough Breaks

Stolen by the Sea

Tulsa Burning

Flying Blind

# HOGGEE

## ANNA MYERS

WALKER & COMPANY
NEW YORK

First published in the United States of America
in 2004 by Walker Publishing Company, Inc.

Published simultaneously in Canada by
Fitzhenry and Whiteside, Markham, Ontario L3R 4T8

For information about permission to reproduce
selections from this book, write to Permissions,
Walker & Company, 104 Fifth Avenue,
New York, New York 10011

Library of Congress Cataloging-in-Publication Data
Myers, Anna.
    Hoggee / Anna Myers.
        p. cm.
    Summary: Always overshadowed by his competitive older brother,
especially in their work as mule drivers on the Erie Canal, fourteen-
year-old Howard finally finds the courage to pursue his dreams of
becoming an educator after he learns about sign language and
teaches it to his deaf friend in nineteenth-century New York State.
    ISBN 0-8027-8926-9 (hardcover)
    [1. Brothers—Fiction.    2. Self-confidence—Fiction.
3. Erie Canal (N.Y.)—Fiction.    4. Deaf—Fiction.    5. People
with disabilities—Fiction.    6. American Sign Language—
Fiction.    7. New York (State)—History—19th century—
Fiction.]    I. Title.

PZ7.M9814Ho    2004
[Fic]—dc22

                                          2004049458

Book design by Jennifer Ann Daddio

Visit Walker & Company's Web site at
www.walkeryoungreaders.com

Printed in the United States of America

2    4    6    8    10    9    7    5    3    1

# DEDICATION

When you came into this world weighing only
one pound and seven ounces, we were so afraid
for you. You were named Paul for your mother's
father, who watches you from heaven, and
Colman for your father's grandfather, who lives
near you in Arkansas. I have always known that
the name Paul is said to mean "little," but since
your birth, I have come to believe it means "little
warrior." You fought hard and well. As I write
this letter you are eight months old, and
miraculously, you have no problems. At not quite
twelve pounds you are still small, but you will
catch up. Your smiles, though, are big, and you
sweetly share them with anyone who looks at
you. Many, many people all over the country
prayed for you, and many people love you. I
hope you will always feel that love. Thank you,
little warrior, for making me a grandmother and
for making my heart sing.

NANA

# CONTENTS

# HOGGEE

# THE WINTER MAY
# KILL ME

The boy sat on the barn floor looking at the words he had carved with his knife on the flat board. The thought had come to him this morning. He had passed the stacks of small boards many times before, but this morning he was taken with the compelling idea of writing his story, of telling the facts of his life. Writing on paper would be easier, but he had no paper. He had no pen. He had no ink. He had only a sudden and demanding need to tell.

A moment had come, when first he settled himself at the task of carving, that he wavered. Who would want to know about a dunderhead such as himself? But, no, the record, he decided, was not so that someone would know. It was because of the need to tell. He traced the words with his finger and bit at his lip. Having written enough for now, he rose to put the board carefully into his haversack.

The movement made the mule, Molly, turn her head to stare at the boy with big dark eyes. "I'm a sorry sight, old girl," he said to her. He touched the cheekbone that stuck from his face and glanced down at the britches, hanging loosely on his body. "It would make my mother cry to see me so thin."

He patted the mule's side and leaned his head against her. "Thank you for sharing your stall with me," he said. He had always loved the mules, but his affection was even stronger now. It was, he knew, the heat that came from Molly's body and from the other mules in the barn that saved him from freezing during the bitter winter nights.

He burrowed back into the pile of straw. His one dirty blanket wrapped tightly around him, he listened to the breathing of the mules and worried. It would likely be starvation that got him. Would it be spring before anyone found him? No, old Cyrus, who came to tend the mules, would eventually notice the smell of his rotting flesh.

He did not know if Captain Travis, who owned the barn and who employed him during the warmer months on the towpath, would have him buried. Captain Gordon Travis was not a man who wasted money. If indeed there was a grave, there would certainly be no marker, not even a crude wooden one. The boy was glad. Any marker would be bound to bear the name *hoggee* with no capital letter. Neither Cyrus nor Captain Travis would know his name, Howard Gardner. To them he was only one of many hoggees, boys paid to drive the mules that pulled the boats up and down the great Erie Canal.

He had hoped to be a worker at O'Grady's Inn for the winter. "It's a dang fool notion," Jack had said, "working for Michael O'Grady, him as mean as a weasel, and you knowing nothing of working in a kitchen. You won't last until Christmas. Then what's to become of you? Come home with me."

It was hard to go against his older brother, but Howard had been determined. On the day he had first talked to O'Grady, things had gone well. He had seen a crudely lettered sign on the inn door and had stopped to stare at the sign. "Kithon Boe Neded," it said. It was their last day before leaving Birchport to go home for the winter. He had been walking past the inn on his way back to the barn.

Maybe he should ask about the job. If he got work for the winter, he thought, he could send all of his hoggee money home, more than Jack would have left to take with him after paying for transportation. Just once, he would be doing something Jack could not do. He walked into the inn.

Three customers sat at a small table eating, and a plump, pleasant-looking woman in an apron stood near the counter. "Excuse me, madam," Howard said to her, and he took off the wool cap he wore. "I've come to ask about the job, the kitchen boy."

The woman looked at him closely. "You know how to work, do you, boy?"

He nodded his head. "I'm a hard worker."

She made a clucking sound with her tongue. "You a hoggee, then?"

For a minute Howard considered lying. Many people looked down on hoggees, the lowliest job on the canal. Often Howard had heard the taunt, "Hoggee on the towpath, / Five cents a day, / Picking up horseballs, / To eat along the way."

But Howard was not a liar. "Yes, madam," he said. "I am a hoggee when there's canal work, but I need something for the winter."

The woman smiled at him. "I expect you'll do, boy,"

she said, "but it's my husband, Mister O'Grady, thinks as he ought to have the say about things around here." She motioned to a table near the counter. "Set yourself down there," she said, "and wait. He'll be along in a wink."

Howard was surprised when the woman brought him a big mug of tea and a slice of freshly baked bread with butter. "Food goes with the job," she said. "Might as well get started." She'll be a good one to work for, he thought. He had just swallowed the last bite of bread when a burly man with a dark beard came in from the back.

Howard jumped to his feet. "He's come about the job, O'Grady," Mistress O'Grady said as she cleared plates from the customers' table. "Seems a likely lad."

O'Grady made a grunting sound and shot Howard one quick glance. "What's your name?" he asked.

"Howard, sir, Howard Gardner."

"Well, Howard," said the man, "the pay's eight dollars a month, but you can eat what's left over in the kitchen and sleep in the back room."

"Very good," said Howard. It was more than he made on the canal. "Do I have the job, then, sir?"

O'Grady nodded his heavy head. "Show up here day after tomorrow morning at seven sharp," he said, and turned to his wife. "Has the butcher's boy been here?" he shouted.

"He has not," said Mrs. O'Grady, and the man stomped away, back into the kitchen.

The woman shook her head and looked at Howard. "He's moody, that one is," she said. "You'll need to learn when it is you need to ignore him and when it is you need to jump out of his way. I'll give you signals when I can." She smiled. "It's me that does most of the cooking, though, so it's me you will be a helper to mostly. O'Grady is fond of staying out front to take the money."

Howard, knowing he could send all his money home with Jack, felt tall and capable. Now he could send his mother extra money, too, something Jack couldn't do. "Thank you, madam. Hoggees are used to being yelled at." With a promise of returning on time, he put on his cap and went out the door. Outside, he put out his hand to pull down the sign with the misspelled words. Something stopped him. Mistress O'Grady had said her husband liked to tend to things about the inn himself, so he decided to leave the sign.

Two days later when he came back and knocked at the back door, it was opened by a boy, one taller and stronger than Howard, with a familiar face that gave Howard a feeling of dread. Howard backed off the stoop. Before him was Mac O'Hern. Mac stepped out onto the back stoop, closed the door, and leaned against the doorpost.

"You're not wanted here, Gardner," he said, his lips twisted into a sneer.

"I am," said Howard. Determined to fight if he had to, he was ready to step back onto the stoop. "I want to see Mister O'Grady."

Mac laughed. "You've seen me, that's seeing enough. You've not got yourself a big brother to fight for you this time."

Just then the door opened wide and Mister O'Grady stood in the doorway. "See to the boiling water, Mac," he muttered.

Howard, relieved, moved back onto the stoop, but

before he could say anything, O'Grady yelled, "Away
with you, you little beggar. I've no use for you. After I
learned your last name, I hired me a decent lad with Irish
blood." He waved his hand and almost struck Howard's
face.

Howard opened his mouth to protest, but the man
gave him no chance. "Don't bother to come out with a
lie. Your da is a bloody Englishman, ain't he?" The man
peered wildly into Howard's startled face.

"Sir," said Howard. "I told you my name. My father's
people were English, but he was born in this country.
Anyway, my father is not alive," said the boy. "He's been
gone these two years now, and my mother, sir, she was
born in Ireland."

"It's a lie," thundered O'Grady. "No Irish lass would
marry an Englishman, and I've no wish to hear sad
tales about your father's death. An Englishman is an
Englishman, as vile in death as in life." He slammed the
door.

Mac had stolen his job by telling O'Grady he was
English. Howard stood on the doorstep. Suddenly the
winter cold cut through his coat, and he began to shiver.
Still staring at the closed door, he backed down the step
and stopped just at the edge of the canal only a few
paces from the inn door. He turned and looked at the
water. It was quiet now. A few days earlier it had been
alive with colorful boats. Shouts from workers on the
line boats that carried freight had filled the air, along
with music and the talk of passengers on the packet
boats. Birchport had bustled then with travelers talking,
arguing, or laughing as they journeyed.

The town seemed strange to him now, and cold,

dreadfully cold. The canal was being drained. Soon it would be almost empty, leaving only enough water so that people could ice-skate. Howard had no ice skates, and he had no business being in Birchport, New York, when there was no water in the canal.

He would find other work. He had to. Jack had gone on the last boat down the icy canal, and even if there had been another boat, he had no money for fares.

For two days he walked about the village, stopping at the taverns, the other inn, the blacksmith shop. One owner after another shook his head. No one in Birchport needed extra help during the winter. Finally at a dry goods and grocery store, he had some hope.

"Our son has up and gone down to the city to work," said the owner. "You can read, you say?"

"Yes, sir," Howard said, "and write a clear hand."

They were discussing wages when the storekeeper's wife came from behind the shelf containing bolts of cloth. Howard could feel her eyes on him. "He's scrawny, Otis," she said, wrinkling her nose. "We can do better. You know we can."

"But he can read and write. Cipher, too," said the man. He looked at Howard. "You can cipher, can't you, boy?"

"Even in my head," Howard said, leaning toward the man. "Twenty take away six is fourteen. Give me bigger numbers."

The storekeeper looked at his wife, and Howard held his breath, waiting.

She frowned. "Otis, we need a boy with a strong back. We'll find one that can lift *and* cipher." She went back to her bolts of cloth.

"I'm stronger than I look," Howard said softly, but he knew there was no hope.

The storekeeper shook his head. "The missus don't rightly take to you, lad," he said. "Lots of canal boys wanting work right now. I'm sorry." Howard turned away quickly, afraid of the tears pushing at the back of his eyes. "Wait," the man called. He cut a piece of cheese from a block on the counter and held it out to the boy. "Here," he said, "take this."

Howard looked back at him, wanting to refuse, wanting to say the man should save the cheese for the strong boy he would hire. "Pay your own way, son," his father had often said. "In this old world, it's best for a man to pay his own way." His father, though, was dead, and the hunger that gnawed at his insides was alive. He reached back, took the cheese, and bolted from the store.

Old Cyrus knew he slept in the barn, had known from that first night when Howard had been turned away from O'Grady's. Cyrus was a crusty old man with gray hair and a long gray beard. He had steel gray eyes, too, and there was no softness in them. He did not like hoggees, but he did like the mules for which he cared. It was because of Molly that Mac O'Hern hated Howard, and it was because of Molly that Cyrus let him stay in the barn.

It had happened before Molly had become Howard's favorite mule, not long after Jack and he had come to work for Captain Travis. Mac had worked for the captain, too, but on a different boat. Mac and Howard happened to lead their mules at the same time into a rest barn. After six hours of duty, Mac was putting Molly away when Howard noticed three open wounds oozing blood on the animal's rump.

He came over for a closer look. "What happened?" he asked Mac.

"Ain't none of your business, as I can see." The boy turned the animal into a stall, fastened the latch, and started to move away.

Howard put his hand gently on the animal's flank, bent to examine the wound, then whirled to see Mac walking away. Howard reached out to pull at Mac's arm. "You whipped her, didn't you?"

"Told you once! It ain't no matter to you."

"It is a matter to me! You've no call to hit an animal that hard." Howard made his hands into fists, but it was too late.

"Maybe you'd rather I hit you then," yelled Mac. His fist collided with Howard's chin, and Howard fell back hard. For a few seconds everything was black. When he opened his eyes, Jack was there, come from the ship that was unloading passengers, and he and Mac were fighting.

Mac was even heavier than Jack and slightly taller. He knocked Jack onto the station floor and jumped on top of him. Howard scrambled to his feet to help his brother, but Jack had already rolled Mac over and was sitting on him.

Jack lifted Mac's head and slammed it hard into the barn's floor. "You want to apologize to my brother now and then dress the wounds on that mule?"

Mac did not answer. Instead he gouged at Jack's eyes. Jack fought him off, grabbed a handful of hair, pulled it hard, then lifted his head by the hair and pounded it twice into the floor. "Now," he said, "have you had a change of mind, my lad?"

Mac said nothing, and Jack lifted his head again. "All

right, all right," the boy muttered. "I'm sorry. Now let me up."

Jack did not turn him loose. "Say, 'I'm sorry, Howard.' And say it like you mean it." He lifted Mac's head again.

"Wait," he said. "I'm sorry, Howard. I really am."

Jack got up then. "Now clean that wound," he said, pointing to the mule.

After watching Mac dress Molly's wound, Howard and Jack went back to their boat. When they stopped at the main barn on the return trip for fresh mules, old Cyrus had demanded to know what had caused the injury to Molly's rump.

Howard, following his brother's lead, had claimed not to know. It was an unwritten law that no hoggee told on another. But they heard later that when Molly kicked Mac hard as he tried to put her in the barn stall, old Cyrus fired him. "When a mule don't like a hoggee," the old man said, "the hoggee has got to go." He scratched his head. "Hoggees just don't be as important as mules in this operation."

Somehow Cyrus had learned the story about Molly and Mac. "You be the one as fought that worthless hoggee over hitting Molly," Cyrus said when he found Howard asleep in the barn.

"I am," Howard answered Cyrus. Then he remembered to give credit where credit was due. "It was my brother who licked him, though."

Cyrus looked at him a minute before he spoke. "Well, you sleeping here, it's no matter to me, boy, but mind you don't let Captain Travis see. It would rile him something fierce, put him in a regulation pucker. He ain't likely to fancy giving hoggees free sleeping quarters of a winter, him having paid you a goodly amount and not wanting to see your face till almost spring."

The boy knew that old Cyrus would rather not have seen his face, either. On the morning of the sixth day, the man questioned him. "You look peaked as a sick baby. Have you filled your belly at all this week, hoggee?"

Something in the old man's voice surprised the boy and made him unwilling to trouble him, so he nodded his head to indicate he had eaten and busied himself with folding his blanket and hiding it under the straw.

After that, Cyrus would bring a leftover biscuit, a morsel of salt pork, or a bit of cold potato from time to time. Once, to Howard's amazement, he brought a molasses cookie. "Don't be depending on me for vittles," the man had warned. "I've got them enough that depend on me, my daughter and her girls. I've no wish to have another mouth to feed." He studied Howard, and he shook his head. "You ain't likely to live till spring, boy."

Howard just nodded. The next morning he began to make marks on the manger in Molly's stall as a record of the days. This morning, before beginning to carve his story, he counted the marks. Six in a row with a seventh across it to mark a week. Four weeks of marks and three more days. So it was December now. Jack would be back in March, when days were warm enough for walking but before the canal was fully thawed. They always walked back to Birchport in the spring. There was no money then for the stage or the canal boat that they used to go home. Besides, the canal boats would not have begun to run yet. They found barns to sleep in on the journey, their feet sore and bleeding by the time they reached the town.

He would be glad to see Jack, but he wondered if he would have to confess about the winter. Would it be possible to deceive Jack, to let him think the winter had passed well? He doubted it. Jack could usually tell when he tried to keep secrets. Besides, his clothing was already very loose. No, Jack would know the truth. He would not chide, would not say blockhead. Instead, Jack would close his eyes briefly and shake his head. That was what Jack always did when faced with Howard's blunders— except, of course, for the fire.

That time, that terrible time when Howard had left a candle too close to a curtain, Jack had yelled at him. When they were all out and staring with unbelieving eyes at the flames, Jack had screamed, "Nitwit! Now you've done it! Where will we live now?"

His mother had cried and said, "Howard, how could you be so careless?"

Even lying there on the floor of the barn, so many miles from his home village, he could close his eyes and draw in that horrible sharp smell that lived in the ashes after the rain fell on them.

Howard was glad then that his father had not been alive to see the blaze. Even his father's patience would have given away.

Howard thought of his father and the gate. At nine, Howard had left the gate open, allowing the cow to wander away to the neighbor's garden. His father had managed, even with the consumption almost finished with him, to walk over to apologize to Mrs. Stempson.

Howard had run for the cow. His father, leaning on the yard post, had closed his eyes, slowly shaking his head. Howard supposed Jack had learned that shaking from their father. "You've got three little sisters will be depending on you. There's a need to grow up now, son," he said. "Like Jack."

Howard had bit at his lip, and his father, aware that his words had stung, had added, "You and Jack both. You've got to hunker down to the business of being men now."

Jack had hunkered down. They had left school that year, Jack gladly, Howard sadly. It had been at school, just a few months earlier, that Howard had experienced something remarkable, something special and sweetly secret. Howard had been at his desk when the schoolmaster stopped to put a hand on his shoulder. "You'll pass your brother in your studies next year, Howard, my boy," the master had said quietly. "You're more of a scholar than young Jack."

A flood of disbelief had rushed through Howard, had filled every blood vessel and made his heart beat wildly. Pass Jack, two years older, stronger, faster, always-at-the-ready Jack! No one had heard the master, Howard's seatmate being absent that day, and Howard had told no one. Sometimes at night while lying in the bed he shared with Jack, he had gone over the scene in his mind, even moving his lips to silently form the teacher's words: "more of a scholar than young Jack."

When the term ended, the teacher had given Howard a book, *The Life and Memorable Actions of George Washington*. Howard had treasured the book; but too self-conscious to show anyone, he had hidden it in the cowshed. After the house had burned, he took it from the shed and said he had found it on the road. He had it now in his haversack, buried under the straw in Molly's stall. After the house burned, though, Howard had no longer gone over and over the teacher's words in his mind. No use to remember kind words. All his hope for the future had burned with the house, leaving him with the unrelenting smell of smoke.

There had been no next year at school for Howard. He had not passed Jack, would never pass Jack. Undoubtedly, Jack would move up in the world of canallers. He could see Jack as a captain, owning his own boat and wearing a smart uniform, waving to Captain Travis. But would he, Howard, have to work, even as a grown man, as a hoggee for his brother? Howard had never known of a hoggee who was a grown man. What became of canallers who did not advance? Maybe they starved during hateful winters.

The days dragged by, one like the other. Sometimes when the wind was not quite as harsh, the boy would leave the barn to wander about the village. Birchport, named for the trees with white bark that grew about the place in abundance, was a true child of the canal. All its businesses faced the waterway, with only narrow strips for carriages. A traveler could step off a boat and be, almost, inside a Birchport shop. Before the canal, there had been no town at all. It was strange to see the empty canal dividing Main Street down the middle.

After a quick walk past the businesses, he liked to go by the academy for boys and even the big stone building with the sign that read, "Phipps Union Seminary for the Education of Girls." Once he crouched behind a bush next to a window that was opened slightly at the bottom. Pressing his ear near the crack, he could hear a girl's voice reading. Howard could not follow the words well enough to understand what she was reading, but he could tell by the rhythm of her voice that it was a poem. Those stolen words were, he knew, as close as he would ever get to being a scholar.

# 2

# I MUST FIND FOOD

Howard was surprised when the hunger pains lessened. He had not known that his body would grow used to not eating. Now his head felt strangely light, and he wanted only to sleep. He knew, though, what his body needed, and he made it part of his carved record.

It became his custom to go at night to the back doors of the inns where he had once sought work. He would stay in the shadows until the leftovers were thrown out, then fight the waiting dogs for bits of food. So he was able to stay alive.

One mild afternoon with no snow on the ground, Howard came upon three girls on the path that led from old Cyrus's house to the barn. They had baskets of walnuts they had picked up from somewhere. Howard was interested. If he could find the tree, there might be nuts left, and his stomach was totally empty.

The girls were dressed alike, in calico dresses, and their long, fair hair was pulled back to hang down their backs. They stopped dead still when Howard approached, and they stared at him with identical big blue eyes. The oldest looked to be about Jack's age, but it was the second tallest who spoke.

"You're him Grandpa says lives in the barn," she said, and her voice was not friendly.

"Yes," he said.

"Leave us alone," the girl said, crossing her arms over her chest. "We don't want nothing to do with you."

"You needn't be so crabby," he said. "I had no plan to disturb you."

The girl who spoke and the younger sister whirled away from him toward the house, but the older girl stood unmoving, staring at Howard, her blue eyes wide. As Howard looked at the girl he saw something in her eyes, something he could hardly bear to see.

This, he knew, was no ordinary girl. He wanted to ask what sorrow filled her heart and spilled over so clearly into those blue eyes. Maybe she, too, had burned her family's home, or, he wondered, could there be something even worse?

Suddenly, the girl who had done the talking turned back and grabbed her sister's hand, pulling her away. The taller girl looked back once over her shoulder. Howard opened his mouth to call to her, but he did not know what to say, so he stood still and watched the girls disappear over a hill.

Howard never found the walnut tree, nor did he see the girls again for a long time, although he watched for them on the path and in the tiny yard around Cyrus's house. He thought often of the oldest girl and wondered about her sadness.

On Christmas morning old Cyrus came early to the barn, amazing Howard with his holiday cheer. "Wake up, hoggee! It's Christmas and it's lucky you are to have lived to see this fine Christmas Day."

Howard awakened reluctantly. He did not feel lucky, and he did not sit up. He had no wish to consider Christmas, did not want to imagine his mother's kitchen, with its wonderful smells and his little sisters smiling.

Old Cyrus poked at the boy with the toe of his shoe. "So is it that you've no desire to get up and face Christmas?"

The boy made no response except to grunt, and Cyrus poked him again. "Up with you," he said. "We've got the matter of Christmas dinner to settle."

Howard, thinking perhaps Cyrus would promise to bring him a bit of food, pushed the straw away from his face and sat up.

"My daughter says it ain't Christian leaving you hungry on Christmas day. She's insisting I ask you to join us for a bit of celebrating," Cyrus said, and he half smiled at the boy. "Captain Travis give me a chicken, he did, and my daughter has made a dressing and beans. Mince pies, too. We've enough to add an extra plate."

Howard stared dumbly at the man.

"Well, boy, speak up. Will you be coming, then?"

"Yes," he said. "Yes, I will."

"There's one more thing." The old man's face was stern again. "It be about my daughter's girls." He took a deep breath. "They ain't, like you'd say, used to company. I don't know as I could recollect the last time someone come in from the outside." Cyrus looked hard at the boy as if he expected a response, but Howard, not knowing what to say, remained quiet. Finally the man went on. "You'd not devil them, would you?"

"I've been taught manners by my mother, sir," Howard said, and Cyrus nodded. Howard wanted to ask about the oldest girl, but he knew Cyrus would not like the question. He would see her again and maybe learn what troubled her.

When the old man was gone, Howard washed his face and hands in the icy trough where the mules drank. Resisting the urge to dry his hands on his dirty clothing, he waved them in the air until they dried. Next he changed into the other clothing he had washed in the trough last week. He took up his comb and ran it through his long, limp hair to comb it back from his eyes. His mother would have been horrified to see him so dirty calling on anyone for Christmas dinner, but he feared the icy water would kill him if he tried to bathe.

When he was dressed, he went outside to the holly tree that grew near the barn. Howard had admired the red berries that grew there earlier, but now he wanted to bring a bit of Christmas inside. He broke some of the thin, berry-laden branches from the tree and took them into the barn. Twisting them together, he made a wreath to hang around Molly's neck. Stepping back, he admired his work. "Merry Christmas to you, old girl," he said. "I'll keep my eye out for a bite of something for your Christmas pleasure." He closed the barn door, climbed the slight hill, and stood looking down at Cyrus's little house behind the large one owned by Captain Travis.

Howard stopped for a minute on the front stoop. He wondered how the second oldest girl would react to his coming. She had been so hostile on the path. He did not wish to offend anyone. But the smell of roasting chicken seeped through the door, and he raised his hand to knock. Before his knuckles hit the wood, the angry girl opened the door.

"Grandpa says you're to come in," she said, and she turned away.

He followed her. The house was small, one main room with two doors opening off of it. Howard supposed those were sleeping rooms. There was a small pantry room off the kitchen, with the door open, and he could see shelves with food on them. A fireplace stood in one corner, but Howard also saw a large cast-iron stove like the one his father had bought his mother for cooking. A long sawbuck table stood near the stove, and there were empty plates on it, and dishes of food. Howard's eyes traveled over loaves of bread and a bowl of beans to a plate of apple slices, once dried and now freshened with water. He would, he decided, slip a piece or two of the apples into his pocket for Molly.

A woman standing near the stove looked up at Howard. "Well, Da," she said to old Cyrus, who sat nearby smoking a pipe, "your visitor has come, it seems. Won't you make us acquainted?"

Cyrus took the pipe from his mouth and scratched at his beard. "This here is my daughter, Mistress Donaldson." Next he pointed to three girls who stood nearby. The one who had opened the door had been joined by the two others, one smaller and one larger. Their hair, clean and dressed in shiny braids, was almost white.

The boy put his hand to his head. His own hair was also that fair, but it was so dirty now that it looked much darker. Cyrus pointed to the tallest girl. "This be

Sarie," he said, and his face warmed with the saying of her name.

"Sarah," his daughter corrected him, but Cyrus paid her no heed. "This be Laura," he said, pointing to the next girl, "and little Grace."

Howard nodded his head to acknowledge the introductions. "Pleased to meet you," he said, but the girls said nothing.

"Da," said Mistress Donaldson. "You've not told us our visitor's name, now have you?"

Old Cyrus twisted his face, thinking. "Why, I don't know your name, boy," he said. "All I know is hoggee, and you ain't rightly a hoggee at the moment, are you? Not in the dead of winter, not on Christmas Day."

The boy nodded. "I'm not," he said. "I'm just plain Howard Gardner."

The woman motioned toward the table. "Set yourself down, then, Howard Gardner. Our Christmas dinner wants eating."

Don't grab, Howard told himself. He wanted to reach out and fill both hands with meat and bread, but he realized the chicken was small. Cyrus passed the platter first to Howard, and he took only a wing. "We'll have none of that holding back, boy," said the man. "It's Christmas now, ain't it?" He used his own fork to spear a thigh to drop onto Howard's plate.

Mostly, he kept his eyes down, happier than he'd ever been to eat any meal. When, occasionally, he did glance up, he was aware of the girls. They sat on a bench across from Howard, and they watched him even as they ate, all three sets of blue eyes stared at him. Two sets were curious, as if he had two heads. The eyes of the older girl, though, were like they were on the path, and Howard looked away from them.

They were, Howard decided, peculiar girls indeed, but he did not let them spoil his delight in the food. His only disappointment was becoming full so soon. His stomach, shrunk as it was, could hold only a small portion of what his eyes wanted.

The last two bites of dressing and beans left on his plate barely went down when he swallowed. Just then Mistress Donaldson took up the mince pie to cut. A small cry rose in his throat. Embarrassed, he choked back the sob. "None for me, ma'am," he said. "I couldn't swallow it."

"What?" The woman looked at him closely. "No mince pie on Christmas? What kind of daft notion is that? Are you that stuffed? You do have a taste for it, though, don't you?"

"Oh, yes, ma'am," he said. "I love it, but I'm hurting from the chicken and all."

"Well, then," she said, "we'll have to wrap a slice for you to tote back with you, won't we?"

Joy filled his heart. He would have mince pie, after all.

"Thank you," he said. "Thank you for the meal, too."

"You're welcome, boy." Mistress Donaldson smiled at him.

The oldest girl followed him to the door. Howard noticed her as he turned to go out. She looked as if she wanted to speak to him, but her mother came, took her by the hand, and led her away, as she would lead a small child.

On the way home, he stopped for a minute, ignoring the cold of the night and looking up at the sky.

"Christmas stars," he said aloud to himself. "Christmas stars." He stared as if he had never before seen such beauty.

Back in the barn, he first gave Molly the apple slices he had slipped into his pocket. While the mule munched, he sat cross-legged in the straw, and very very slowly he ate his Christmas pie.

# 3

# I HAVE A FRIEND

Howard carved his third message a few days after Christmas. Cyrus had gone immediately back to his cranky ways, and the boy was not invited again to his house. Once, just after a fresh snow, Howard saw three sets of footprints, and knowing they belonged to the girls, he followed them over a hill.

A small frozen pond lay at the bottom of the hill, and the girls skated there. They looked carefree and happy. Howard wanted to watch them, but he knew the girls would object. A cedar with low green branches grew halfway down the hill. While they were turned away from him, he dashed for the tree and slid in among the branches.

They were good skaters, gliding easily around the pond. The oldest of the three was especially graceful. Her legs seeming to move without effort, she was a willowy streak, her fair hair flying out behind her and shining in the winter sun.

He was not surprised to see that Sarah was different from her sisters. They laughed and called to each other as they skated, but Sarah seemed unaware of them. Watching, Howard remembered how it had been the middle girl, Laura, who had spoken to him on the path. It had been Laura, too, who opened the door to him on Christmas Day. Howard knew from his life with Jack that the oldest child was always the leader at home. Something, he decided, was wrong with the girl Sarah. She must not be right in the head, addled. Yet, she didn't seem disturbed. He hurt for the skater, who moved so beautifully but had to be led by the hand of her mother or sisters.

He knew he should leave, go back to the barn or to the tavern to wait for scraps, but he was reluctant to move. At one point, Laura stopped skating and went to a basket they had set beside the pond. She took out bread and pieces of meat. This time both Sarah and Grace skated to her, and Laura handed out food to them.

Howard had not tasted food at all that day and had eaten only a few scraps from the inn the day before. His mouth watered with hunger. The girls seemed to have plenty, and he wondered if they would share if he called out to them. But remembering how Laura had acted toward him, he doubted it.

As they ate, bits of conversation drifted to him, but he could not understand any of their words. Once, the girl Sarah turned suddenly. For a split second, Howard felt her eyes on him. He dropped behind the tree, hoping she had not really seen him.

Not long after that, they left. He saw that Sarah had forgotten her muffler, left lying on a rock where they had stood eating. Deciding to retrieve the muffler and take it to the girls' mother, he was about to leave his spot behind the tree when Sarah ran back for the muffler. She looked for a long moment toward the tree where Howard hid. Then she lifted the muffler from the rock.

In its place she laid a slice of bread and a piece of meat, which she removed from her coat pocket.

"She knows I'm here," he whispered to himself in amazement. "She knows I'm here, and she wants to give me food." He stepped from his hiding place and called to her. "Sarah." She did not look up at him as she took up the muffler and hurried away. Just before she disappeared among the pine trees on the other side of the pond, she stopped. Turning back to stare across at Howard, she stood still for a moment. Then she lifted her hand and waved it slightly.

Howard, too, lifted his arm to wave, but she was gone; like a startled deer, she ran into the trees. For a long time he stood staring after her, wondering.

Back at the barn, he took up his board, opened his knife, and carved. It felt strange, writing that he had a friend. There had been playmates at school when he was younger and boys on the canal with whom he had joked, but a friend was different. Howard believed that somehow he and Sarah had communicated, had acknowledged each other's suffering. He felt a strength grow inside him that had not been there for a long time. Looking down at his carved message, he drew himself up to sit very straight.

Sarah's gift was all he had to eat that day. At the inn, Howard waited in the cold shadows for a long time. Finally, the cook opened the door and threw out a plate of scraps, mostly crusts of bread. When the door closed, the boy sprang toward the food, but suddenly two big dogs blocked his way. Howard spotted a piece of potato worth fighting for. In a flash he bent, grabbed up a handful of stones, and tossed them at the animals. They growled without even lifting their heads to look in his direction.

In a matter of seconds, all morsels of food had been swallowed up.

On the way back to the barn that night, he lingered even longer than usual, looking at the lamplight streaming through the windows of old Cyrus's house. Inside was Sarah, the strange girl who had wanted to share her food with him. That did not seem to be the action of a girl whose mind was not right. He would get up his courage, he decided, to ask her grandfather about her.

Usually Cyrus woke him as he entered, but the next morning Howard was awake under the hay, waiting. The old man had refused Howard's help with the hay in the past. "It's my job and my wages," he had said when Howard had taken up a pitchfork and started to fill a manger. "I'd sooner you left the haying to me."

Howard had not tried to help again. Nor was Cyrus inclined to conversation other than an occasional muttered greeting. Usually Howard burrowed back under the straw after sitting up to see for sure that the person in the barn was indeed Cyrus.

This morning, though, he got up and followed the man to the last of the ten stalls where Cyrus always began the haying. Cyrus, ignoring the boy, began to fill his pitchfork with hay. He had just tossed the first load into a manger when Howard got up his courage. Clearing his throat, he said, "I saw your granddaughters yesterday, skating on the pond."

The old man whirled, pitchfork still in the air, to look at the boy. His blue eyes flashed with fire. For one second Howard thought Cyrus might use the pitchfork as a spear, to slice through him and fasten him to the earthen barn floor. "I told you," he said strongly, "they ain't used to people." He drove the pitchfork into the ground, hard. "Leave 'em be. I won't have you deviling them."

Howard stepped back. "I didn't," he said quickly. "I didn't devil them at all, didn't even call out to them." He took a breath to slow the beating of his heart and the speed of his words. "Cyrus, I would never hurt them— just watched, that's all. They are good skaters."

The old man stared at him a minute, then repeated his warning. "Leave 'em be. If you don't, I'll turn you out of this barn to freeze. I will, by thunder! You just watch and see if I don't."

Despite the cold, Howard's forehead was sweating. He ran his hand across it before he spoke. "I will never cause them trouble," he said. "I promise you, Cyrus. That's not the way I am. Remember how I took up for Molly?"

Cyrus peered closely into Howard's face, considering. "Well," he said, "you do seem a good-hearted lad." He shrugged his shoulders. "Maybe I got too riled up." He swallowed hard. "I got to protect them, that's all. They got no da to do so, and it's all up to me. I got to protect them, most particular Sarie."

Howard, leaning against a mule stall, knew he should let the conversation go at that, but he couldn't.

"What's wrong with Sarah?" he asked.

"There you go!" Cyrus stuck the pitchfork back into the hay. "That's the way it starts! I won't have her stared at and poked at." He turned to face Howard. "She ain't right, boy. That's all you need to know. She ain't right, and it's done broke her mother's heart. You leave her be. Good-hearted or no, you can't help her none. I shouldn't never have agreed to have you in at Christmas, shouldn't never have looked the other way concerning you staying

the winter here in this barn, you with no work to oc-
cupy you."

"I won't bother her," the boy said, "nor question you
again, neither. I'm sorry." He went back to Molly's stall
near the front of the barn, dug down to cover himself
with straw, and stayed there until the man was gone.

# 4

## MY FRIEND IS
## EVEN SADDER
## THAN I AM

Howard carved the words by the light of a candle he had found in the barn. It was not easy to light the candle even though there had been pieces of flint and steel beside it. Howard had to strike the flint to get a spark, light a string, and finally get a blaze from the candle. It was not a process he wanted to go through often. Besides, it made him nervous to have even a small candle in the barn with so much hay. Howard had reason to worry about fires.

Still, he had to have light, had to carve. The day had begun by his studying the marks on Molly's stall. They told him that it was the middle of January—a new year—1838. He only had to survive two and a half more months until his brother's return. It would not matter that Jack would fume over Howard's bad decision. He would be in charge again. Jack would make sure that Howard was never hungry again. His brother always knew what to do.

Then life on the canal would begin again. Being a hoggee was hard, driving the mules for six long hours without a break, sleeping on the boat for six hours, and going back to work again. No one could call it easy, but as a hoggee Howard's stomach had been well filled. Captain Travis knew he got better work from well-fed hoggees, just as he did from well-fed mules.

Old Cyrus had brought him nothing yesterday, and the boy worried that Cyrus was too angry over his questions about Sarah to ever give him another morsel of food. Tonight he would have to fight the dogs for the scraps. He stayed in the barn until after dark. The wind cut cruelly through his thin coat, but he lowered his head and pushed himself to move ahead. On the curve of the road, he paused for a minute to look at Cyrus's house. Just as he turned half away, his eyes caught sight of a girl holding a large candle in front of the window.

"Sarah," Howard said aloud. She turned to the side, and he could see the outline of her nose and of her chin. He could see the long hair that hung straight behind her back. "Sarah," he said again softly.

Howard wanted to knock at the door. He wanted to speak to Sarah. In the darkness he could not see her eyes, but still he felt her sadness. He was alone, hungry, and cold. Sarah lived with people who cared for her, but somehow he knew that she too felt alone. Her sisters had been unaware of his presence as they had skated, but Sarah had known he was there. She knew, too, that he was hungry, and she cared. Her actions were not those of a demented person.

Too cold to stand still longer and too touched by Sarah's sorrow to go on to town, he went back to the barn to carve. Later, when his need to record had been satisfied, he went back outside to move toward the town. It was early in the evening, but few people were on the streets.

Snow had begun to fall, great fat flakes that quickly

covered the wooden walks the merchants had cleared from earlier snows. On the way to O'Grady's Inn, Howard passed only two men and a woman, their heads down to shield their faces from the wind. Customers at the inn would be few this evening. He feared there would be no scraps.

Hope, though, grew in his heart when he reached the back of the establishment. There were no waiting dogs. They're too smart to be out on a night like this, he told himself. They're hunkered down somewhere out of the cold. It was just then that he saw something not usually there, a large wooden whiskey barrel. O'Grady must have emptied it and thrown it out the back door.

Howard rolled the barrel away from the light that came through the back windows. Then he crawled inside. The strong whiskey smell made him slightly dizzy, but he was much warmer. Here he could wait. Surely there would be something thrown out. Before long the door opened. Howard could see Mac there in the light, and he watched as the boy threw out a plate of something.

When the door closed, he crawled out of the barrel and, without getting fully upright, moved quickly to the scraps. On the snow were several scraps of bread and two small pieces of meat. Howard's heart raced, and he dropped to his knees to retrieve the food. So thrilled was he with his good luck that he did not know the door behind him had opened again.

Suddenly, he knew he was no longer alone. The light from the open kitchen door revealed Mac running toward him. Howard dropped the scraps and scrambled to get to his feet, but Mac was too quick. His fist struck Howard's face hard, and the boy rocked back on his knees. Mac leaned down, grabbed his shirt, and yanked Howard up so that he could hit him again. Howard fell to the ground, terribly aware of Mac's heavy boot coming toward him. Howard tried to roll, but the boot caught him. When the first kick struck his stomach, he cried out in pain. Mercifully, something in his head seemed to switch off before the second kick, and he felt nothing when the boot struck again.

His head cleared for a second, and a thought flashed through his mind. This is the end. I'll die tonight. I won't starve, after all. It was not a particularly frightening thought, just one of certainty. A call came then from the open door. "Stop it," a woman shouted. "Stop it right now, or I'll come at you myself with this butcher knife." Even in his terrible confusion Howard knew the speaker was Mistress O'Grady.

"Ah," said Mac, his tone surly, "the little beggar hankers to be taught a lesson or two." He turned, though, and went back inside the kitchen.

Unable to move, Howard lay for a time in the snow. He thought of crawling back into the barrel, but Mac might find him there. There was, he knew, no way he could make it all the way to the barn, but he had to get away from O'Grady's. He put his hands down in the snow to push himself up to his knees.

It was then that he found it, a small leather purse lying in the snow. He opened the purse and found a ten-dollar gold piece and a silver dime. Howard sucked in his breath with surprise. Still on his knees, he glanced over his shoulder. No one from the inn watched. He slipped the purse into his pocket.

I've got to run, he thought. I've got to get out of here before Mac comes back. The purse had probably

come from Mac's pocket, and he would miss it at any
moment.

Keeping something that did not belong to you was
stealing, wasn't it? He should return the purse, but he
knew he would be beaten again. Besides, hadn't Mac
stolen his job? The money in that purse would be more
than enough to feed him through the rest of the horrible winter.

He pushed himself up and staggered away from the
inn's back door. As Howard passed the backs of the dry
goods store and the blacksmith shop, his head hurt and
he felt dizzy. But he pushed himself on, determined to
get farther away from Mac. Next was the livery stable,
where people paid to have their horses kept. Pausing
there to lean on the building, he saw a crack of light
shine through the back door. Probably someone was
sleeping in a room inside to take care of travelers' horses.
Maybe he should open the door and say, "Please, sir,
may I lie down here for just a bit?"

He reached out his hand toward the door. I'll pull it
open ever so slightly, he told himself, but his hand did
not grasp anything. It slid, instead, down the wood, and
Howard's body slid also. He lay there, unconscious in
the snow, for a very long time.

Then someone shook him. "Wake up, boy!" a voice
demanded. "You're nearly frozen. Wake up, I say."

Howard opened his eyes and tried to struggle to his
feet. "Whoa there, now," said the voice, and Howard saw
a man hunkered down beside him. "Let me help you."

The man stood; then taking Howard's hand, he pulled
him to his feet.

"Thank you, sir." Howard leaned against the
building.

"Where do you live, boy?" He pointed to a horse and buggy that stood just outside the livery stable. "I'll give you a lift home."

Howard looked at the man, and his head cleared enough to think straight. The man's clothing did not look expensive, but he was dressed nicely enough, and he did have money to keep a horse and carriage. He might know Captain Travis. Howard knew he should not tell him that he lived in the captain's barn, but he needed that ride badly. "I'm boarding with old Cyrus," he said, realizing he did not know Cyrus's last name. "He takes care of Captain Travis's mules."

"I know Captain Travis's place. I'll take you there," said the man, and he helped Howard climb up to the seat. He took a blanket from a chest beneath the seat and wrapped it around the shivering boy.

They moved through Birchport in the darkness. For a time they rode in silence. Then the man spoke. "I was just bringing my rig in," he said as he drove. "I've been on quite a journey to visit my mother, and got delayed when my horse threw a shoe. I think my bad luck was your good fortune."

Even in the darkness, Howard could feel the man's eyes on him. His teeth had stopped chattering some, and he was able to say, "Yes, sir. I might have frozen to death if you hadn't come along and found me."

"Well," said the man, "boys are my business. I teach over at the academy for boys."

Howard made a grunting noise to acknowledge that he understood.

"My name is Thomas Parrish," the man said. "Will you tell me yours?"

"Howard Gardner."

"Do you go to school, Howard?"

Howard swallowed before he spoke. He did not want his voice to be full of self-pity. "I did go to school, sir, but my father died. I'm a hoggee now. Well, not now because it's winter."

"I wonder if you will tell me why you were lying out in the snow on such a night?"

Howard sighed. "I got whipped, beat up in a fight, and I guess I passed out."

"I see," said the man.

Howard wanted to explain. He did not want Thomas Parrish to think he was a ruffian. "The fight wasn't my idea, sir. The other boy attacked me."

"I see," the man said again.

They rode on in silence, and soon the rig turned off the road onto Captain Travis's property. "Cyrus lives just over the hill," Howard said, and then he felt embarrassed. "I didn't mean you had to drive me to the door, sir. Of course I can walk."

Thomas Parrish put out his hand to touch Howard's arm and urged his horses on. "No, Howard, I am not at all sure you can walk. I'll take you to the door."

Now Howard felt panicky. He could not go into Cyrus's house in the middle of the night. He had to tell this man that he slept in the barn. "Well, sir, I don't so much sleep in the house. I've got a nice cozy little room in the barn."

The man nodded. "The barn it will be, then." When he stopped, he said, "Wait now, let me help you down."

"Thank you, sir," Howard said when he stood on the ground. "Thank you very much."

Thomas Parrish nodded again and climbed back onto the buggy. "You go on in, Howard," he said.

"I'd like to see you inside before I go."

Howard turned to move slowly toward the door. He had taken a few steps when he felt compelled to stop and turn back to the man. "I have a book," he called. "*The Life and Memorable Actions of George Washington*. That's the name of it, and I have read it many times."

"I'm glad, Howard," said the man. "I am glad you have a book."

Howard dropped his head and turned away to go inside the barn. Why had he told Master Parrish about the book? What difference did it make that some hoggee owned a book? "You didn't tell him you started a fire," a voice inside his head said. "You didn't tell him you burned your mother's house." He pushed his way through the barn door, closed it behind him, found Molly's stall, and burrowed into the straw to find his blanket.

It was then that he remembered the purse. Holding his breath, he jammed his hand quickly into his pocket. "Oh," he said aloud when his fingers closed over the clasp, "it's still there." Something made him decide to bury the purse. Using his last bit of strength, he dug with his knife to make a shallow hole, put in the purse, and patted dirt back over it. He crawled under the hay with his blanket and went quickly to sleep.

Howard slept fitfully. The next morning, Cyrus muttered a greeting as he took Molly from her stall to put her in the exercise lot. Howard managed to grunt in response. His head hurt fiercely, his mouth was as dry as cotton, and he felt feverishly hot. He thought of asking Cyrus to get him a drink, but when he opened his mouth no words came. His head swam, and he dropped back into a troubled sleep.

When he woke next, he knew he had to have water. Somehow, he managed to crawl from beneath the hay and inch his way to Molly's water trough. Usually he drank from the pipe where clean water first ran into the barn, but the entry pipe was across the barn. Now he made no attempt to avoid drinking with the mules.

He pulled himself up to the trough, lowered his head to the water, and drank. His face burned with fever. He wanted to use his hands to splash water onto his hot cheeks, but when he let go of the trough to do so, he fell back onto the barn floor. Exhausted, he drifted back into sleep.

In the evening, Cyrus found him there beside the trough. "Boy," he said to him, "boy, wake up." Howard did not respond. Cyrus touched his red face. "You're on fire with fever."

Howard opened his eyes slightly. "Water," he managed to say.

"I'll fetch you a drink." He went to the entry pipe, took down a tin cup that hung there, and filled it with water.

Howard tried to sit up as he heard Cyrus coming back to him, but he could not. Cyrus lifted his head so that he could drink. "Thank . . ." He closed his eyes and could not finish.

"You're sick, lad," Cyrus said, "real sick. I'll get my daughter and the cart." He hurried from the barn.

When he came back, he pulled a wooden cart. Mistress Donaldson came, too. She knelt beside Howard, put one hand on his forehead and one over his heart. She made a sad clucking sound with her tongue, then said, "This boy is near dead, Da."

"I know, daughter. Help me lift him into the cart."

Howard was aware of their words and of being lifted. The cart had low walls. They folded his legs tight against his chest to squeeze him in. "'Tis only a short ride," Cyrus said, and Howard felt the cart begin to move.

"I can walk," he murmured as they pulled him out of the cart, but when they let him try to stand, his knees buckled.

"Girls," called Mistress Donaldson, and her two younger daughters came running from the house. One girl and old Cyrus lifted his head and shoulders; the other girl and her mother carried his legs. They took him to the tiny pantry off the kitchen. A feather mattress had been placed on the floor, and they laid Howard on it.

He slept for a moment. Then Mistress Donaldson knelt beside him. Using a wash pan, she washed his face with a cloth, and the water felt cool and wonderful. Next she removed his shirt to wash his chest and arms. "He's in need of a doctor, Da," he heard the woman say. "We can't stand by and watch the lad die, now, can we?"

"It will cost dearly," Cyrus said with a sigh, "still there's nothing for it but to send Laura to fetch Doc Pruett."

"Send Grace along for company," said the woman. "Tell them to hurry."

Howard tried to speak, too, to say that he had money for the doctor, but the thought never fully formed in his mind. He drifted instead into a strange dream in which Mac knocked at the door of Howard's home to complain about his missing purse. In the dream Howard's mother scolded him loudly for stealing and said she was glad his father had not lived to learn his son was a thief. Howard stood in a corner beside the stove like the one in Cyrus's house, and he felt his face hot with shame. Jack came in, and he fought with Mac. When Jack had beaten Mac badly, Cyrus and his daughter came and took Mac away in a cart.

It was Dr. Pruett who woke him. "Boy," he said, "can you wake up and talk to me?"

Howard heard the voice, but it seemed very far away and unconnected to him. "What's his name?" the doctor asked.

Without opening his eyes, Howard became aware of Mistress Donaldson kneeling beside his bed. "Let me think now," she said. "He told us at Christmastime."

"It's Howard," said a girl's voice from a little farther away.

"You're right, Laura," said the woman. "Howard it is."

"Howard," said the doctor. "Howard, open your eyes and talk to me."

His eyelids felt so heavy, but Howard strained to open them. The young doctor leaned over him and said, "That's right, Howard. Come on, now, wake up. Do you hurt anywhere, Howard?"

"My chest feels . . ." A cough rose up from inside him and shook his body.

When he was quiet, the doctor took a thermometer from the black bag that sat beside him. "Here," he said. "Close your lips around this."

The doctor pointed to the bruises on Howard's body and face. "He's been injured," he said, "badly injured." Next he took a stethoscope from his bag, fastened the tubes into his ears, placed the round part on Howard's chest, then listened. "Congestion," he said, more to himself than to the listeners. He took the thermometer from Howard's mouth and held it up to read. "He is burning up," he said, nodding to Mistress Donaldson. "This boy has pneumonia." He shook his head sadly.

"What's to be done for him?" Cyrus asked.

"Not much, I'm afraid. Give him water, and cool his face and arms with a wet cloth." He took a bottle from his bag. "Try giving him a drink of this once in a while. It might help cut the phlegm."

"You'll bleed him, though, won't you?" asked Mistress Donaldson.

Howard heard her, and he opened his mouth enough to get out, "No," but they did not seem to hear.

Doctor Pruett was getting up and reaching for his bag. "I don't believe in bleeding," he said. "Most doctors today agree it only weakens the patient."

Mistress Donaldson pursed her lips. "Old Doc Conklin bled my mum, he did, and she had pneumonia."

Young Doctor Pruett smiled. "And did your mother recover?" he asked.

"She did not," said Cyrus. "Leave the doctoring to the doctor, Mary."

"This boy may not live, either," said the doctor, "but if he doesn't, it won't be because he is too weak from loss of blood to fight the disease."

"What's to be your fee?" old Cyrus asked.

"You have taken the boy in from the goodness of your heart," said the doctor. "I'll not be charging you to boot."

"We can pay," said Cyrus.

The doctor shook his head. Then his eyes fell on the table and an apple pie still warm from the oven. "I'd be pleased, though, to have a piece of that pie."

For the rest of the day Howard slept and woke, slept and woke. Mistress Donaldson brought him cups of water to sip from. The boy was amazed to wake once and find old Cyrus washing his face. No one else was around, and the old man talked to the boy.

"I never had me a son," he said, "nor a grandson. I don't know as I've ever washed a boy's face before, not since I washed my own."

Howard wanted to say thank you, but he was too tired.

Young Grace brought him a pillow. "Here," she said, and she lifted his head to slide the pillow beneath it. "You can have my pillow. I don't need it much."

It was Laura who spooned a bit of broth into his mouth. Howard was aware when the lamps were blown out, and the family went to bed.

Sometime during the night, he woke. Someone was pulling the blanket up around his shoulders. He opened his eyes. It was Sarah. Next she lifted his head and helped him drink a few sips of water. The girl sat beside him until he went back to sleep, but she did not speak a word.

# 5

# I KNOW NOW WHAT
# BURDEN SARAH BEARS—
# I WISH I DID NOT

It took Howard a long time to learn what caused Sarah's sorrow. He lay on his feather mattress, spending his days and nights in strange dreams. Outside, the wind howled and snow swirled. After a week or so, Mistress Donaldson began to feed him spoonfuls of soup instead of clear broth. "I believe you're going to live, Howard, boy," she said after the first soup was swallowed.

Sometimes he was confused and thought that Mistress Donaldson was his mother. Old Cyrus frequently knelt down to put his hand on Howard's forehead to check his fever. "You're not so hot," he declared one day, but Howard still felt as if a fire raged somewhere inside him. He still coughed, too.

At night, Howard often thought of the light that would be shining out the window into the darkness. He was inside the house now, but he still felt lonely. It was the youngest girl, Gracie, who first began to visit him for no reason. She would push open the pantry door, grin at him, and close the door.

On the third time he was ready for her. "Want to hear a rhyme?" he said when her head appeared.

She cocked her head, studied him for a moment, then came into the room, plopped down cross-legged on his mattress to wait.

"Hey diddle, diddle, / The cat and the fiddle, / The cow jumped over the moon, / The little dog laughed, / To see such a sport, / And the dish ran away with the spoon," Howard said, and Gracie laughed.

"You aren't a ruffian," she said. "Grandpa always told us hoggees be ruffians."

"Well," said Howard. "Maybe he meant other hoggees. I don't suppose he would let me sleep in his house if I were a ruffian, now, would he?"

Gracie smiled and nodded. "Very well," she said. "I will be back to listen to more rhymes." She got up then, and without another word, she left the room. Then she stuck her head back in briefly to make a funny face, her eyes bulging out, her nose and eyebrows twitching.

Each day Howard had another rhyme ready for her. Then one day Laura stood in the doorway with Gracie. She looked at the floor. "I don't have a lot to do right now," she said, and she shrugged her shoulders. "Mayhap I will pass the time along with Gracie listening to your rhymes."

Gracie came in, settled on the mattress, and Laura pulled a kitchen chair into the tiny room.

"How about a riddle instead?" he asked when they were ready.

Laura frowned. "I don't know what *riddle* means," she said softly.

Surprised, Howard pushed himself up to rest on his elbow. "It's a mystery, like a question for studying out the

answer. Here's one. 'Runs all day and never walks, /
Often murmurs, never talks, / It has a bed and never
sleeps, / It has a mouth and never eats.'"

Thinking, Laura twisted her face, and in just a moment, understanding flashed into her eyes. "Oh, I
know!" She clapped her hands. "River! It's a river."

Howard smiled and lay back on the mattress. "You're
quick," he said. "Why don't you go to school?"

Laura shook her head. "Grandpa doesn't hold with
girls getting schooling. He thinks reading and writing
wouldn't do us no good. He says me and Gracie will
just grow up and get married, and it don't take learning
to do that."

"What about Sarah?" he asked. "What will become
of her?"

Laura scooted closer, then leaned toward him.
"Sarah helps mother," she said very softly, and she
looked over her shoulder. "Don't let Ma or Grandfather
hear you asking such. They'd be awful vexed."

Howard nodded. He lay back on his mattress and
thought. What was wrong with Sarah, and why were
the grown-ups determined that he should never talk to
her? He was almost certain that her mind was not bad.

He had seen Sarah carrying in firewood, and he had
seen her clearing the table after family meals. She had
never spoken to him. Then he realized that he had
never heard Sarah say anything to anyone in the family.
Even with the thin door closed, he could hear them talk
at supper. Now that he was better, Howard frequently
listened to the conversation. Old Cyrus talked mostly of
the weather and of the mules. Mistress Donaldson spoke
of what she had seen or heard at the village market.

Laura and Grace made small comments about their daily lives. Only Sarah remained always silent.

After the day of the riddle, both of the younger girls began to spend more time with Howard. Even before he was well enough to sit up, he liked to talk to them until he grew too tired. He told them about Molly and about his family. He did not tell them about burning the house. He remembered it often, though, the smell strong in his nose.

For a long time he did not speak about Jack. He felt, somehow, that telling them about Jack would be the beginning of losing their friendship, as if anyone who knew about Jack could not value Howard. Yet it seemed disloyal not to mention Jack at all. Then one day he forced himself to talk about his brother. "Jack's the oldest," he said. "Jack is strong and quick. He always does what's right and doesn't make blunders." Suddenly a memory came to Howard, and he smiled. "Well," he said, "Jack did get fooled once.

"It happened during that year after our father's death before we left for the canal. I got tired sometimes, Jack forever telling me what to do and being perfect. It was my job to gather the eggs, but one day I didn't do it. I stayed behind the henhouse until I heard my mother call out the door for eggs. 'I'll fetch them,' I heard Jack yell. 'Howard's gone off somewhere.'

"There was a tiny crack in the henhouse wall. I had pushed through a strip of black cloth into the first hen's nest. Through the crack, I could just make out Jack's form reaching into the nest, and I pulled the cloth at just the right moment.

"'Snake!' yelled Jack, and he jumped back, dropping

an egg. I yanked the cloth hard back through the crack and stuffed it in my pocket.

"'I'll help you,' I called, and I ran around the hen-house and went inside. Jack had a hoe ready to kill the snake, but it had disappeared.

"'I'm not sure there was really a snake,' I told our mother that night at supper.

"'I didn't imagine it,' Jack said, and he glared at me.

"I couldn't let it go with Jack not knowing that I had put one over on him. That night I put the strip on Jack's pillow and waited for him to pull back the cover. 'Snake!' I cried, and I broke into laughter. Jack, of course, caught on at once. He had a dipper full of water from the drinking bucket, and he threw it on me. I didn't mind being wet, not one bit."

Howard raised himself up on his elbow. "If you meet him in the spring, it might be best if you don't mention snakes in the henhouse." He laughed. Then he grew serious. "Jack would never have let himself get down sick this way."

"People fall sick," Laura said. "It wasn't your fault."

"It *is* my fault that I ended up cold and hungry instead of warm and fed at my mother's house, and that's what weakened me so the sickness could come over me."

"Well," said Laura, "I'm glad you got sick." Her face reddened. "We should never have known you if you hadn't."

Howard, unaccustomed to kind words, turned his head toward the wall.

"I don't want to meet Jack," said Gracie.

"Gracie," said Laura, "that's not nice to say."

Gracie frowned. "I think Jack ain't very interesting, being always right." She shrugged. "We won't meet him, anyway, on account of Sarah."

Howard pushed himself to sit up. "What do you mean?"

Laura frowned at Gracie and turned to Howard. "Grandfather and Ma don't like to have people around us because Sarah is the way she is. They say folks will point at her and make fun."

"What's wrong with Sarah, Laura?" he asked. "You can tell me."

"We're not supposed to talk to you about her," said Laura. "Gracie shouldn't have mentioned about your brother not meeting us. We've got chores to do," she said. She got up from her chair, took Gracie's hand, and pulled her little sister behind her.

Gracie looked back at Howard, and she made a funny face.

Howard stared after them. When he got a chance, he would ask them again. If Laura wouldn't tell him, he was pretty sure Gracie would.

They did not come back until after supper. When he opened his eyes after a nap, Gracie sat cross-legged on the mattress beside him. "You been missing that mule Molly a good bit," she said, her round blue eyes dancing. "So I've been going down to the big barn, and learned to sound just like her." She put back her head, screwed up her face, and let out a bray.

Howard laughed. He had not laughed for a very long time. The sound rang strangely in his ears, but with Gracie around he became used to laughter. One evening he was awakened from a nap by a rush of cold air. He sat up. The windowpanes were open, and cold air was coming into the room between them. Howard didn't think he could stand up to go to the window. He remembered that Gracie had lifted the latch that held the two side panes together earlier to open the window for a minute. He supposed she had forgotten to put the latch back securely, letting the wind blow the window open.

"Gracie," he called, thinking he would ask her to come back into the room to close the panes.

"Yes," her voice answered from outside the window.

Then a snorting sound came through the window. Something bumped against the glass, and Howard, thinking the little girl had found something to climb up on, expected to see Gracie's head poke into the room. Instead, a brown muzzle with a strip of white on it appeared in the window. Then Molly's whole head appeared.

"Molly!" said Howard, and he crawled across his mattress, pulled himself partly up with a pantry shelf to steady him, and stretched up his hand to pat the head.

"Ma had a conniption when I tried to bring Molly in the house," Gracie said from below the window. "Ma is real persnickety about mules and houses." Howard was too weak to pet Molly more, but he smiled all evening.

Even with Gracie to entertain him, the days were long. He missed making the notches in Molly's stall. He was better now. The coughing had almost gone, but he was weak still. He could sit up for a short time, leaning against the wall beside his mattress, but he could not stand. He wondered how long it had been since he had been transported from the barn on that small wooden cart.

One day when old Cyrus brought him a cup of milk, Howard asked, "How long have I been here?"

"Umm, let me think now." He sat down on a kitchen chair and scratched his beard. "It's been a good while now, two fortnights maybe."

Howard put down the cup he had started toward his lips. "That's a month! Is it February already?"

Cyrus rubbed his chin. "Well," he said, "maybe. I mostly let the canal and the trees tell me the time. Not a trace of spring to be seen. That's a fact. When the ice starts to break up a bit and the green things first bud out, the hoggees will come drifting back to work. That will be spring."

"I'll be strong enough to go back to the barn soon," said Howard. "Tomorrow I'm going to try to stand, and I'll try walking."

"There be no hurry, boy. We're mostly used to you now." Then he laughed. "Molly, though, she misses you a good bit. Looks behind me, she does, when I come in, and shakes her head in disgust."

Howard spent a lot of time worrying about the money. He wanted to go back to the barn. He wanted to see if the money was really under the hay. Sometimes he thought finding the purse in the snow had been part of the strange dreams brought on by the raging fever. He wondered what he would do with the money. It was not his, and he knew he should return it, but to whom?

Finally, he decided he would take just enough to buy a little food until spring. The rest he would return to Mistress O'Grady. She would know what to do with it. He felt better.

The next day he did stand. Laura and Gracie helped, one girl holding to each of his arms as he pushed himself up against the wall. His breaths came heavily, and his knees shook.

"Ma says it's being in bed so long makes you weak," Laura said. "She says you'll get your strength back a bit at a time."

He nodded, then let his body slide down against the wall. "Thank you for helping," he said when he had caught his breath. He stretched across the mattress. "I'd like to try again, later, if you could help me again," he said.

They said they would, but Howard grew tired of waiting. He decided to try by himself. He rolled to the wall, sat up against it, and began to struggle to push himself up. Something made him look toward the door. Sarah stood there in the doorway, watching.

"Hello," he said.

The girl said nothing. She looked at him for a moment. Then she came toward him, walking across his mattress. She took his arm and began to pull upward until he was standing.

"Thank you, Sarah," he said.

For a moment she stared into his eyes, then she turned and ran from the room. "Sarah," he said. "Sarah, wait." She did not look back.

The next day it happened again. He had just started to push himself up when he felt her eyes upon him again. "Sarah," he said. He spoke softly, hoping not to scare her away, but then Laura appeared beside her. She took Sarah's hand and pulled her away.

He stood leaning against the wall for a moment and

had just started to slide down when Laura came back. She stood in the doorway, her arms folded across her chest. "Leave Sarah be," she said. "I told you Grandpa would be fit to be tied was he to find you bothering her."

Howard let himself slide down to sit on the mattress with his back to the wall. "I wasn't bothering her," he said. "She just stopped in the doorway, and I spoke to her. That's all."

Laura let out a deep breath. "You can't talk to Sarah," she said, "and she can't talk to you."

"Why?"

"She can't hear, and she can't talk." Tears began to well up in her eyes and run down her cheeks. "She wasn't born that way. Ma says it came on her after a terrible fever when she was about a year old. They didn't know she couldn't hear until our da accidentally dropped a big crock on the floor behind her. He yelled, too, but Sarah just sat there in front of him and never looked his way. She's lived most of her sixteen years now never hearing a thing. Grandpa says folks would poke fun at her if we was to take her places, and he don't like company to come into our house. You're the first one ever."

"Deaf and mute," said Howard.

"Yes," said Laura, "now you know. Ma has taught her how to work some by pointing and such, but that's it. She ain't right, that's all, and you've got no call to be worrying her by trying to talk to her."

Howard nodded. "I won't try to talk to her again."

"Good," said Laura. She turned and left the room. That night Howard woke to a strange sound. It came from the main room, and after a moment he realized someone was crying. He crawled to the door, pulled himself up in the doorway, and looked out into the dark room.

Someone sat on the kitchen bench that had been moved to be beside the window. Moonlight came through the window, and Howard could see that whoever was crying was too big to be Gracie; it had to be Laura or Sarah. The sobs were loud and strange, and he realized they came from Sarah.

He had never heard such a sorrowful sound, such desperate crying. He wanted to go to the girl. He wanted to comfort her, but how could he?

Leaning against the wall, he made his way to the kitchen table. He would hold onto it and be able to walk to the bench where Sarah sat.

Howard breathed hard. He lifted his feet as little as possible, saving his strength. Knowing she could not hear him, he tried to think how to let her know he was there so she would not be frightened when she saw him. He looked around the room. A broom stood near his door, and he made his way back to get it. Then when he had inched forward enough, he held the broomstick out to touch Sarah's shoulder.

She turned to see him. Howard thought she might run, but she didn't. She sat very still and watched him move toward her. She had stopped sobbing, and she wiped at her eyes with her hand. She wore a heavy flannel nightgown and a white ruffled cap like the one his mother wore for sleeping.

There was room for him on the bench beside her, and he almost fell onto the spot. For a moment they sat

quietly. Then Sarah scooted away from him and began
to cry again. Howard reached out and touched her
hand. She turned to look at him, then got up and hurried away into the bedroom she shared with her mother
and sisters.

For a while Howard sat on the bench and stared out
into the night. The heaviness he so frequently felt inside had grown. Now he no longer felt sad for himself.
Sarah's sorrow was so much heavier.

Two days later he went back to the barn. Old Cyrus
had made him a walking stick, and he leaned heavily on
it when he had to stop to rest. Laura and Gracie walked
with him. Gracie carried a lunch of bread and cheese
she had tied up for him in a cloth. Laura stayed close
beside him in case he needed help, but he was able to
walk alone.

"It will be strange, you not being in our pantry,"
Laura said when they were inside the barn door. Gracie
made a face, and he laughed.

Molly was glad to see him. He went to her and
stroked her neck. "You don't scratch a mule's ears," he
told Laura and Gracie. "Horses like that, but not
mules." The girls did not stay long. As soon as they
were gone, Howard thought of the purse. First he dug
under the straw. There was the pebble that marked the
spot. He took his knife from his pocket, opened it, and
used it as a digging tool. In a moment his fingers
touched the material of the purse, and he could feel the
money inside. He covered it again with a little dirt and
the pebble, put the straw back on top, and stretched out
on it for a nap.

When he woke, he took one of the small boards

from the stack. Words pushed up from inside him, and he used his knife to release them. After he had written about Sarah's grief, he expected to feel better, but he didn't. He sat leaning against the boards in Molly's stall, remembering the sound of Sarah's crying.

# 6

## I AM A TEACHER

They were, Howard thought when he had carved them, magnificent words. Words he had never supposed would be said of him, and he carved them with absolute joy.

For two days he had stayed in the barn or at least close by. Using his walking stick to help, he moved about until he was exhausted, then fell into the straw to rest. Laura and Gracie brought him food. The first afternoon they stayed. After he had eaten, Gracie went off to play in the haystack. Laura and Howard stretched out in the straw, and Howard told her about his life on the canal. "We've been hoggees for three years now. I was eleven and Jack thirteen when we started. I never took to the canal the way Jack has. He loves it, but I'd find another way to live if I could. Still, I think the canal is interesting. We've walked on every mile of the towpath, all three hundred sixty-three of them between Albany and Buffalo, through mountains and valleys and swamps. Sometimes when they first open the locks in the spring, I stick my hand in the water that's come down from Lake Erie. I watch the water separate and go around my hand. I think how the same water that touched my hand will keep going till it gets to Albany. The water will go all the way down the river to New York. Then it will go into the ocean. Water that touched my hand will go into that great sea."

"Oh," said Laura. "That makes you part of the ocean, sort of. I would love to see the sea."

"Me, too," said Howard. "I surely would love to go with that water that touches my hand."

The next afternoon he read to them from his book about George Washington.

"Was he a friend of yours?" Gracie asked.

"No, he lived a hundred years ago," said Howard.

"Oh. Want to see me stand on my head?" Gracie asked.

"Gracie," said Laura, "you know Ma told you to stop standing on your head. She says your brain will get topsy-turvy. Besides, every bit of your pantalets would show. It's not nice to show your pantalets to boys."

Grace nodded her head and stared at Howard. "Oh, that's right. Howard is a boy. You're the first boy we've ever talked to."

"I'd like to be able to read and write," said Laura, and she reached out her hand to touch his book. "Do you think you could teach me?"

Howard bit at his lip, wondering. He wasn't sure how a person went about teaching someone to read, and there was another problem. "Do you think your grandpa would object?" he asked.

Laura nodded. "He will object, but mayhap I can persuade him. He doesn't want me going to school because he thinks it's a waste of time, but you teaching me wouldn't take so much time away from my chores. I've heard him talk of the brothers he left in Ireland when he came to this country. I'll bring them up, tell him that if I can write, I'll send letters to see if any of them can be found. Grandfather can sometimes be softened, and I believe Ma would be made glad by me learning."

"I don't think I want to learn to read," said Gracie. "I think that reading might make my brain all topsy-turvy."

After two days in the barn, Howard felt strong enough to walk to town. He took his stick to lean on, and he took the purse. He used the canal bridge to cross Main Street and get to O'Grady's Inn. He stood outside the window and looked at the sign. Below the letters were pictures of a bed and of a table with dishes on it. Signs like that, Howard knew, were for people who could not read. If he did not teach her to read, Laura would need such signs all her life. What about Sarah? What would become of her after her grandfather and mother were gone?

He shrugged his shoulders. He could not spend time right now worrying about Cyrus's granddaughters. He had to worry about himself. Right now he needed to find the courage to go inside the inn. If Mac saw him, he might get beaten up again. He didn't want to encounter O'Grady, either, but standing a few feet away, he was not close enough to see who was in the dining room. He would have to get closer.

He edged his way toward the window. Finally, his nose touched the glass. He put his hands up around his face to block the light from outside, and he could see into the inn. Two tables had customers, and Mistress O'Grady stood behind the counter. O'Grady or Mac could be in the back. They could come in at any minute. He drew in a deep breath and stepped toward the door.

Mistress O'Grady looked up as he entered. Howard

walked across the room, his eyes always on the door that
led to the kitchen. "Hello," she said when he was beside
the counter, "Ain't you him that O'Grady promised the
job to, then went back on his word?"

Howard nodded. "I am, but I've not come to cause
trouble." He leaned closer to her. "I've a matter to talk
to you about, but I'm concerned . . ." He paused and
looked toward the kitchen door.

"Well, boy, there's no one in the back if that's what
bothers you. I've sent that rascal Mac off to the butcher's;
won't be back for a while. O'Grady's poorly and gone
upstairs to bed."

"It's about this purse," Howard said, and he drew it
from his pocket. "I found it the night Mac fought me
behind this place. Remember you called him off of
me?"

"Aye, I recollect. Wasn't sure, though, it was you."

"It was, and I am beholding to you, but it's the purse
that brought me here. There's money in it, and I
thought you might see that it got returned to the
owner." He held the purse out to her. "I'd have been
here sooner, but illness slowed me."

The woman made no move to take the purse. She
leaned her plump arms on the counter. "See here, boy,"
she said, "I wouldn't be a-knowing who lost that purse."

"I thought it might be Mister O'Grady's or maybe
Mac's."

She shook her head. "Either of them lost a purse with
money in it, there would have been plenty of noise
around here about it. Besides, Mac is a bully and a
thief." She laughed. "My husband, well . . ." She shook
her head and reached out to push Howard's hand back
toward him. "You keep the purse, and its contents, boy."

"Are you sure?" he asked.

"I am. Now set yourself down over there. I've just enough stew left to give you a nice bowl."

The stew warmed him, and he felt stronger and more confident. Just as he was going out the door Mac appeared. Mac pushed his way through the door and made a sort of sound like the growling of the hungry dogs. Howard wanted to run, but instead he looked Mac in the eye and continued through the door.

He had given some consideration as to how he would buy food and had decided to ask old Cyrus about paying to eat with the family. It was growing dark by the time he walked from town. Might as well go in now, he told himself. Cyrus would be in the house after having finished his evening chores.

Light from the lamp came out the window. This time it did not make him lonely. He knocked, and Gracie opened the door. "It's Howard," she called. "Mayhap he's sick again."

"You sound hopeful," he said to her. "Do you wish me sick again?"

Gracie grinned. "It was a frolic," she said, "having you in the pantry." She stepped aside for him to enter.

"Well, I'm sorry, then, to tell you I'm a little weak still, but fit enough to walk to town." He followed her inside.

Old Cyrus sat at the table smoking his pipe, and the girls cleared the table. Mistress Donaldson dipped hot water from a large kettle into a dishpan that sat on a small cook table beside the stove. "We've just finished," she said, "but there's a bit of beans left in the bowl, I believe."

"Thank you, but I'm not hungry," he said. "It's food I've come to talk to you about though."

"Set yourself down then, boy," said Cyrus.

Both Laura and Gracie stopped what they were doing to listen to the conversation. Howard looked around for Sarah and saw her standing in the doorway to the bedroom, where the shadows almost hid her from sight.

"I found some money outside O'Grady's Inn," he said. "I tried to give it to Mistress O'Grady, but she said I should keep it. It's enough to pay you for taking care of me and, if you're willing, for eating with you until I go back on the boat."

Cyrus smoked his pipe, and Howard waited for him to think about the offer. Laura came and put her hand on her grandfather's shoulder. She said nothing, but Howard knew she had something she wanted to say. "As to your sickness, I've no wish to take your money for doing what any Christian ought," he said. "But there is a bit of work you might do in exchange for stopping at our table now." He patted Laura's hand. "My granddaughter here says how you're powerful good at making out words. She has a hankering to do the same, and she's persuaded me to let her try. Laura's of the mind that you could teach her." He blew out his smoke and looked at Howard. "Well, are ye able?"

Howard smiled. "I don't know, sir, but I'd like to try."

Cyrus stood up. "Well then it's a deal, a lesson after each meal."

Howard spent the last days of winter concerned with two things, teaching Laura and walking to the canal. He knew it was too early for water to be let back into it, but it would not be long. Seeing the canal on the first day became important to him. He wanted to plunge in his hand, hold it under as long as the cold would allow, then pull it out to know the water would go on to the sea.

The wind was not so cold now. He wandered about the village and found a shop that had a few books. "Do you have a reading book?" he asked the woman behind the counter. "One that a beginner would use?"

She shook her head. "I'm afraid you can't teach yourself to read from a book, lad."

"No," he told her. "I want to teach someone else."

"Oh." She nodded and turned to the shelf behind her. "This would do." She handed him a book. *The Eclectic First Reader for Young Children* was the title, and it was written by a man named McGuffey.

"Yes," he said. "This will do nicely." He bought the book, a writing tablet, a quill pen, and some ink. A calendar hung on the wall, and the shopkeeper told him that the day was the last day of February.

Howard loved holding the book, loved walking back to Cyrus's house with it tucked under his arm. Laura loved it, too. He laid the paper, pen, ink, and quill on the bench beside him while he ate, but he had hidden the book under his shirt before going in.

After the meal Howard waited while the girls cleared the table. When Laura sat down beside him at the table, he pulled out the book and put it on the table in front of her. "It's for teaching you," he said. "You're going to learn from the same book they use at school."

Laura sucked in her breath with surprise and joy. "Oh," she said, tracing the letters on the cover. "I never hoped to see a real schoolbook."

He opened the book and read the lesson to her. Laura was quick to learn even that first night. Back at the barn, Howard carved his sixth message and felt better than ever he had in his life—except for the time the master said he was a better scholar than Jack.

Each day Howard taught Laura and was amazed at her progress. After going over the previous list, they would read the last story again, then turn to a new lesson. They worked on writing too, starting with the letters of her name.

Each time Laura read, her finger touching every word, Howard would look up to see Sarah standing in the doorway of the bedroom, watching. He knew she could not hear their voices, knew she could not learn anything by watching. Her face, though, held an intent look, as if she were trying to concentrate enough to somehow grasp the meaning of the words in the book.

They were working on lesson six when Howard could no longer stand Sarah's face so full of longing. "I'm going to move," he told Laura, and he pushed the book so that he sat on the other side of her, away from seeing the bedroom door.

"It troubles you, Sarah watching," she said. "It weighs on me, too. All my life I've ached considerable over having what Sarah never can have." She sighed. "It pains me bad."

Suddenly Howard thought of Jack. Did Jack fret over being so much more able than his younger brother? He wanted to see Jack, wanted to hear about his mother and the girls, but he did not want to answer Jack's questions about the winter. He did not want to see that look in Jack's eyes.

He had thought that perhaps he would lie to Jack

when he returned next month. Maybe he would pull the purse of money out and tell Jack that he had saved the money from his wages.

Laura had her finger on the words in lesson six. "You must not lie," she read. "Bad boys lie, and swear, and steal."

Howard almost laughed aloud at the coincidence. He looked down at the words. He would not lie. He would not be a bad boy. He went back to listening to Laura. "When you fall down, you must not cry, but get up, and run again. If you cry, the boys will call you a baby."

Howard nodded. "Very good, Laura," he said. "You are an excellent scholar." He could no longer see Sarah but knew she still stood just across the room. She still watched. He knew that when he left the kitchen to walk back to the barn, tears would push from his eyes to run down his cheeks. There would be no other boys to call him "baby."

After learning the date on the day he bought the book, Howard had gone back to making his notches on Molly's stall. It was the evening of March 10 when he first saw the water. After the evening lesson with Laura, he walked down to the canal. The moon shone brightly, and the wind was not bitter. The canal had water in it! He bent low over the water to watch the way light from the stars sparkled in the canal.

A great sigh of satisfaction came from him, and even though the ground was still cold, he dropped to sit for a while on the bank. Drawing in the fishy, wet smell so familiar to his nose, he stuck in his hand and watched the waters from Lake Erie separate and move on to the sea. Soon the sound of spring frogs would fill the air, and he would be back with the mules, walking along the towpath. The rhythm of their feet falling solidly on the hard mud path was a sound Howard now realized he loved. It would be good to be back at work.

Jack came back the next day. Howard heard the barn door open that evening just before dark, and he knew who it was even before he saw his brother. He could feel Jack's presence, and he felt both anxious and reassured.

Howard had already settled down for the night with his blanket under the straw, and he came crawling out just as Jack walked in. The light inside the barn was dim, but it was not yet dark outside. Jack looked so tall, so strong, standing there with the light behind him. Had he grown so much during the winter? Maybe Howard had forgotten how big his brother was.

For a moment Howard stayed quiet. Jack would not expect him to be in the barn. He would think he was still sleeping at O'Grady's. Hoggees would be coming back for the next few days to sleep in the barns before they were assigned to a boat. Last year Jack and Howard had both been assigned to the packet boat *The Blue Bird,* but Captain Travis also owned two other packet boats, *The Yellow Bird* and *The Red Bird.* What if they were not assigned to be on the same boat this year? It might feel good not to have Jack watching him always, but then there would be no Jack to take up for him in the fights that always erupted at the locks. There would be no Jack to make him laugh.

Jack came in, took his haversack from his back, and dropped it near the door. There was food inside, and

Howard knew Jack would have to keep the bag with him after the others boys arrived. Most of the boys were hungry and would not hesitate to steal Jack's food.

Howard brushed away the straw and stood up. "Jack," he called, "over here."

"Howard?" Jack waited for Howard to come to him, but Howard did not move. Jack came to stand beside Molly's stall.

Howard stepped out of the stall. They punched at each other's arms, both grinning. "How's Ma?" Howard asked. "And the little ones?"

"Ma was real put out with you for not coming home. She said to tell you not to do that again, said she didn't need money so bad as to have you stay here all winter just to spare your travel money."

Howard looked down. "Well, I won't be tempted to work for O'Grady next winter. That's for sure."

"Didn't fare well, did you?"

"O'Grady gave the job to Mac."

Jack closed his eyes and shook his head. "How did you live, then, all winter with no job?"

"I got another job." Howard took his own haversack from the rail where it hung on a nail. He opened the pack and brought out the reader. "I'm teaching old Cyrus's granddaughter to read."

Jack frowned. "He pays you for that?"

"I eat with the family." He started to tell Jack about the purse and the money, but he decided not to. Perhaps he would tell him later.

Jack looked closely at Howard. "You're thin," he said.

"I got pneumonia. Mac beat me up pretty bad, and I stayed for a long time in the snow. After I got sick, they took me in at Cyrus's house."

"How sick?"

Howard shrugged his shoulders. "Pretty sick, I reckon. They had the doctor and all." He shrugged again. "I'm fit as a fiddle now though."

Jack closed his eyes again, let out a sigh, and shook his head. "It's a thousand wonders I found you still alive."

Howard turned away. "Want to get your bag and sleep in here with me?"

Jack laughed. "No," he said, "I'm not sleeping in there with a mule. I don't trust her not to kick me or step on me."

"Molly wouldn't do that." Howard laughed. "Not unless you riled her."

"I'm not taking any chances." Jack turned to go back to the front of the barn. "I'll find a spot up front. Come on with me. I'm near about starved."

Howard followed. Jack dropped to the straw-covered barn floor, opened his haversack, and took out a cloth that had bread and meat wrapped in it. He tore the bread apart and held out a piece to Howard. "Want some?"

Howard shook his head. "I had plenty for supper." He stretched beside his brother.

"At old Cyrus's house?" Jack smiled. "Eating at old Cyrus's house, if that doesn't beat the Dutch! Remember how he always told us hoggees that he would fire any one of us that happened to be caught even close to the path to his place?"

Howard frowned. "He doesn't like people around his granddaughters. That's all. One's deaf and mute, and he's afraid she'll be made sport of."

Jack took out his pocketknife and cut himself a piece of meat. "Deaf and mute." He shook his head slowly.

"Can't hear or say a word. That's awful sad. How old is she?"

"Sixteen, same as you."

"I'd like to see her."

Howard sat up straight. "She's not a sight in a sideshow," he said, and anger filled him. "That's just what Cyrus doesn't want, people staring at her like she's some freak or something."

"Whoa, now. I never said I thought she was a freak. Don't be so vexed." Jack laughed. "Sounds like you're a little sweet on this dummy."

Howard clenched his fists. "That's crazy," he said. "I just feel sorry for her, that's all, and I'm beholden to old Cyrus. I shouldn't have told you about Sarah. I just want you to stay away from her, you hear? And don't call her a dummy."

Jack stared at Howard. "Don't get yourself all riled up," he said. "I've no plan to plague the girl."

Howard searched his mind desperately for a change of subject. "Want to play marbles?" Howard asked.

"It's too dark for marbles, dunce." Jack cocked his head and continued to stare. "What is it with you? You've never volunteered to play marbles. I've always had to hound you to get a game."

Howard felt his face flush. It was true. He did not like to play any game with Jack, who always won. He did play, though. Partly he supposed it was the hope of winning. Partly he played because he had no power to resist when Jack insisted.

He swallowed hard. "Are you tired, then? You've been on a long journey. Bet you're ready to go to sleep." He started to stand, but Jack pulled him back.

"Not sleepy yet, just got aching feet. Tell me more about old Cyrus's house."

Howard sighed. "Not much to tell. It's just a little house. I had a bed in the pantry while I was sick. Cyrus's widow daughter lives with him and her three girls. It's the middle one I teach."

"How old is that one?"

"Fourteen, like me."

"Are they pretty?"

"Who?" said Howard.

"Cyrus's granddaughters, of course? Who were we talking about? The mules?"

Now Howard was really angry. "How would I know if they're pretty? I don't think about such things! Now mules I can tell you about, but not girls. I don't know about girls, and I don't talk about them. Ma wouldn't like you talking about them, either."

Jack laughed. "There's nothing wrong with saying whether a girl's pretty or not!"

Howard did stand this time. "All right!" he said. "I suppose they're pretty enough, but that's no matter to us or anyone else. Cyrus means for them to be left alone, and you had best abide by that." He stomped away. Then he turned back to call to his brother. "I'm going to bed," he said. "I'm too tired for such non-sense."

In the quiet of Molly's stall he thought about what had just happened. Jack was interested in girls now. He was interested in Cyrus's granddaughters. The thought made him uncomfortable in a way that the hardness of his bed never did.

He did not want Jack to go around Sarah and Laura.

In the darkness he bit at his lip. Jack would not be cruel. Howard had never known his brother to hurt anyone except boys like Mac, who started the trouble. "So what are you worried about?" he whispered to himself in the dark.

He turned in his blanket. Admit it, he thought, you don't want to share Sarah and the others. If Jack gets to know the girls, he will find a way to turn that knowing into a competition. With Jack that's how everything ends, a competition that Jack always wins.

Howard opened his eyes in the morning as Cyrus came in. For a second he forgot that his brother also slept in the barn. Then it came to him. This would be a day of contests. He drew in a deep breath and sat up.

"Good morning, sir," Jack said to Cyrus, and Howard saw him jump to his feet. "I'll be glad to help you with the chores."

Howard smiled, knowing what would come next.

"Don't want help," Cyrus said, and he picked up the pitchfork. "I'm paid to take care of the mules. You're paid for driving them. I don't try to drive them. You don't try to tend them."

Howard thought of crawling back under the straw, but Jack had already seen him. Jack came to Molly's stall. "I've got some bread and dried apples, want some?"

"No, you'll need your food. I'll eat at Cyrus's house when he finishes his chores."

"Right, I forgot. I'll eat later, too. I've got a new sling. Let's go and try it out."

Howard sighed. He had no interest in using Jack's new sling, but he took his haversack from the nail. "I'll take my book and paper, and go from out there up to breakfast."

Outside, the new March morning was crisp, and
Howard pulled his coat closed. Jack showed his sling.
"Isn't this something?" He held out the leather strap
and pointed at the pocket where two leather strings
held a small rock. "Will, the tanner, made it. I worked
for him four days to pay for it. Watch this," he said.
"See that fence post?" He pointed toward a post several feet away. "I can hit it." He began to swing the
strap in a wide circle above his head, then pulled one
of the strings, and a rock flew across the field, striking
the post. "It's how David killed the giant, you know, in
the Bible."

Howard did know about David. He knew that it had
been David, not his older brothers, who brought down
Goliath. He also knew that Jack was going to insist that
Howard now try to hit the post. "You're good with
that," he said. "I guess you've practiced a lot."

"Some," said Jack, "but it's pretty easy." He walked
toward the post. Howard followed. Jack bent to get his
rock. "Here," he slipped the rock back into the pocket,
walked back a ways from the post, and handed the sling
to Howard. "Make it circle above your head. Pull the
string when it's lined up with the post."

Howard began to circle the strap above his head. He
watched the post and pulled the release string at what
he thought might be the right time. The rock missed
the post by several feet.

"Not bad for the first time," yelled Jack, and he ran
to get the rock. "Here," he said, handing the rock to
Howard. "Let's put it back in so you can try again."
He was smiling. "When you're better, we can have a
competition." He stood back, waiting for Howard to
swing.

For just a minute Howard hesitated, but he knew he would work to learn the sling. It was always this way— Jack smiling, Howard dreading. Howard felt powerless when it came to his brother. He would, he supposed, follow always behind Jack, always losing and always, always trying again.

He was still swinging the sling, still trying to hit the post with the rock when old Cyrus came out of the barn. "I've got to go," Howard said, and he handed the sling to his brother.

"We'll practice some more later," Jack said, and of course Howard nodded.

"That lad's your brother, aye?"

"Yes." Howard did not add any comments. He did not feel like talking about Jack.

"He's a likely lad, I'd say. Should make his way well in the world."

"Yes," Howard said again. His feet began to feel very heavy.

Cyrus stopped, looked up at the sky, then turned his gaze to look around at the trees. "Might say spring is here. The other lads will be showing up in the next few days."

"I'll have to go on the boat," said Howard. "It will make me sad to leave Laura's lessons."

Old Cyrus shook his head. "It's no matter," he said. "A girl ain't in need of book learning."

"She wants to learn," said Howard. "I know how she feels. I'd like more schooling myself." He put out his hand to touch the man's arm. "Is there any chance you might send Laura to school?"

"No," said Cyrus, and he shook off Howard's hand.

"Don't bring it up again. I won't have you stirring the girl up with such nonsense."

"I won't say anything," said Howard. He looked down at the ground.

When breakfast was over, Laura helped her mother and Gracie clear the table. Sarah disappeared as soon as the meal was finished. Howard spread the reader open and took out paper and pencil. They went over the word list from the day before, and he wrote sentences using some of the words for Laura to read. As they worked, he glanced often at the bedroom door. What, he wondered, did Sarah do in her spare time? When she was not working with her mother, what occupied her mind and her hands?

The lesson was almost over when he looked up to see Sarah. She stood in the bedroom doorway, just as she had during other lessons. Howard took up the pencil and wrote a sentence for Laura. "She is sad," he wrote.

─────〰〰〰─────

# 7

# JACK WINS, ALWAYS

H e carved the words in the moonlight. It was not a
new idea. Howard had been aware of Jack's winning as long as he could remember. Still, the words stung
as he carved them, stung with a new sharpness. This
contest had mattered so much more than the others.

For a few days Howard and Jack had waited. Other
boys also returned, ready to go back to work as hoggees.
When Howard was not at Cyrus's house eating or teaching Laura, he was practicing with the sling. "You're getting good," Jack would say. And he was improving.

Howard lowered the sling he had started to twirl.
"Well, then," he said, "we may as well have the competition and get it over with."

Jack shook his head. "No, I want you to have a real
chance of winning."

Howard threw up the sling again. It was always that
way. Jack took no pleasure in beating him easily. Occasionally, Jack would even let Howard win, but Howard
was not fooled. He knew that Jack feared he would get
discouraged with no victories at all. Jack need not have
worried. Howard could no more walk away from Jack's

competitions than he could turn his back on water to drink.

Once, last summer, Howard had actually won a race, and he knew from the look on Jack's face that Jack had not given the success to him. For a few minutes Howard had been exhilarated, but the thrill did not last long. Jack insisted they race again immediately. Howard bent his legs in the starting position. You beat him once, he told himself over and over, but he knew he could never do it again. Jack, newly determined, reached the finish line well ahead.

"We'll have to have the slingshot competition tomorrow," Jack said one evening when Howard came back to the barn after his lesson with Laura. "We're going to work tomorrow. Captain Travis was here while you were gone."

Howard stopped in the barn doorway. "It doesn't seem warm enough. We're going day after tomorrow?"

"Yes." Jack sat up from his straw bed. "You and Bert Briscoe are hoggees on *The Blue Bird.*"

"We're on different boats!" Howard walked over and dropped down beside Jack. "Why'd he put us on different boats? He knows we're brothers."

Jack held out his hand in a stop motion. "Whoa! I never said we're on different boats. I said you and Bert are the hoggees on *The Blue Bird.*" He stopped and smiled big before going on. "I'm to be a bowman this year." Jack punched Howard on the shoulder. "I've been promoted, little brother!"

Howard stared at his brother. "A bowman, not a hoggee? I thought bowman were grown men."

Jack laughed. "I'm sixteen," he said. "It appears that is

man enough for Captain Travis." He pulled himself up
to sit very straight. "He said he had been keeping his eye
on me. Liked my work, that's what he said."

"You'll make more money," said Howard. "Ma will
be glad of that."

"That I will, twelve dollars a month and less work to
boot. I can tell you I'd rather see to that towrope than
drive the mules. All that money, and all I have to do is
keep that rope clear of tangles."

"You've got to secure the boat in the locks, too," said
Howard.

Jack smiled. "I like the locks, always have."

Howard liked the locks, too, watching the water being shut in or let out to move the water to a different
level of the landscape. There were always interesting
things going on at the locks, too. Drivers had a chance
to hear stories told by the lockmen and watch fights
over one boat slowing another one down. Howard was
careful not to be involved in the fights, but Jack sometimes took part.

That night Howard lay awake in Molly's stall for a
long time. Jack had started his climb. Howard had
known it would happen, but he hadn't expected it quite
so soon. From bowman, Jack would probably move up
to being a helmsman and then a captain. Howard remembered old Cyrus's words: "Your brother is a likely
lad." Everyone noticed. Jack was apt to be a captain before he was twenty. He would undoubtedly be the
youngest captain on the Erie Canal and be written about
in newspapers and history books.

Howard went to sleep thinking of Jack in his handsome captain's uniform, blue with gold braids. He imagined the boat pulling away with Jack on the deck,

waving good-bye to people at the canal's edge. He saw himself, too, on the towpath as usual. He would be driving Molly as always, and he would be watching for flowers to fasten in her harness.

Howard dreaded telling Laura that their lessons were about to end. He said nothing during the morning lesson, but he did push her more than usual. "Let's do two lessons this morning," he said.

After the noon meal, though, he knew he should tell her the truth. "This is our last day," he said when the table was cleared. "I go back to work tomorrow on *The Blue Bird*."

The girl's eyes grew wide. "But I don't know very much," she protested. "I want to learn more."

Howard felt guilty, then irritated. He wasn't responsible for this girl's education. "I guess that's how it goes," he said, and he frowned. "I never wanted to leave school, either, but here I am. I guess what we want doesn't have a lot to do with what happens." He took the reader from his haversack and slammed it down on the table.

"I'm sorry," said Laura. "I had not meant to sound ungrateful."

Howard softened. "It's all right," said Howard. "I understand how you feel." An idea came to him. "How would you like to keep this book? You could work your way through it, I think. You are getting good at sounding out words."

"Keep your book?" Laura reached out to touch the cover and then put her hand over Howard's. "You would let me keep your book?"

Laura's touch sent a new but pleasant sensation through his hand. For a second he did not remember what they were discussing. Then he came to himself.

"Yes," said Howard, and he gave his head a decided nod. "You can keep the book. The paper and quill, too. I bought it all to use with you."

"You've been a good friend to me, Howard Gardner." Tears came to her eyes, and she moved her hand to wipe them away. "Mayhap I'll never find a better friend."

Howard felt his face grow warm. "I wish I could do more," he said. It was then that he saw Sarah, as always, in the doorway, and he said what filled his mind. "I'd like to help Sarah, too." He nodded his head in her direction. "It must be very lonely in her world."

"Oh, yes," said Laura, and her voice almost broke. "It must be very lonely indeed, but what could you ever do to help Sarah?"

"I don't know." He shrugged his shoulders. "Maybe nothing, but I'd like to very much. I wonder what will become of her."

Laura lowered her voice as if Sarah could hear. "Mother says someday both Gracie and I will marry and move out of this house." She shook her head. "I won't, though." She pressed her lips together. "I could never go away and leave Sarah. With me and Gracie gone, she would be too alone and silent."

On the way back to the barn, Howard thought about the sisters. Gracie was young and frolicked through her days, but Laura worried about the future. Laura felt bound by her silent sister, just as he felt bound by Jack. Laura would live her life trying to make up for Sarah's limitation, and Howard would live his life trying to compete with Jack. Neither of them would ever succeed or break free.

So deep in thought was he as he followed the trail to the barn that he failed to notice old Cyrus. The man stood in the woodlot near the path. He had loaded pieces of firewood onto a mule-drawn cart, and he waited for Howard to approach him. "Boy," he called as Howard walked by. "I've something to tell you," he said, and he moved closer to Howard. "I've been thinking about your brother," he said, "and I told my daughter to set an extra place at the table tonight." He paused for a second and then went on. "It being your last night with us and all, I thought why not have your brother, too. I figure he's running low on rations by now."

Howard was amazed. This was not at all like Cyrus. Then a thought came to him. "Did you hear about Jack's good fortune?"

"Aye, I did." Cyrus leaned against his cart. "Captain Travis told me, he did. Bowman at such a young age! I knew he was a likely lad! Didn't I say as much to you just the other morn?"

Howard nodded. "You did."

"Well," said Cyrus with a smile, "you bring your brother around for supper. My daughter and her girls will be happy to have him for company. We'll have a bit of celebration for his good fortune."

"I'll bring him," he said, and he walked on. So Jack would meet Cyrus's granddaughters, after all. Howard kicked at a stone. Nothing could ever be just his, not with Jack around. He frowned. Obviously Laura wasn't the only one thinking about her future. Her grandfather, Howard felt certain, was thinking it might not be too soon to introduce her to a "likely" young man. The idea made him feel sick to his stomach. It would, of course, be a while before Laura was of an age to marry. By that time Jack would be a helmsman for sure, and on his way to being a captain.

Jack was inside the barn playing marbles with Bert, one of the other hoggees. They had just drawn the lag line and were shooting their taws in that direction to see who played first. "Want to play with us?" Jack asked, but Howard shook his head.

Howard watched Bert first rub his big marble between his hands. "I warm her up this way," he said, but his shot missed the line.

Jack took his taw up, got up on one knee to shoot, and sent his marble to rest almost on the line.

"That does it," said Bert. "You shoot first."

"Oh good," said Jack. He looked up and smiled as if he were surprised to have done so well. Howard felt an urge to yell out, of course Jack shoots first! There was never any bloody doubt! Jack always shoots first. Jack always runs faster. Jack always twirls a sling best. Jack always flies his kite highest. Jack is always liked best by girls' grandfathers.

But he did not yell out. He said nothing. He walked back to Molly's stall even though she was in the exercise yard. Usually he could not turn away from Jack's contest, even when he did not participate, but this time he forced himself. He took out his book, settled himself in the straw, and tried to read. Sounds of the game, though, came to him from across the barn, and finally he gave in to the urge to go and see. Two other boys, Roger and Andy, sat on the straw watching.

Howard counted the marbles in each boy's pile. Bert had two more marbles than Jack. Bert's ahead, thought

Howard, but Jack will come from behind. Jack loved coming from behind to win a game.

"My turn," said Jack. He got up to choose a shooting spot on the other side of the ring. Howard felt confused, not knowing what to hope for. Wouldn't it be good to see someone beat Jack? His brother, Howard knew, would be a good loser, congratulating the winner warmly, but Howard also knew Jack would hate losing. Did he want to watch his brother meet defeat just once? Yes, just once it would be fun.

Jack smiled as he aimed, but Howard noticed the smile was tight, not lips open as usual. Kneeling on one knee, Jack touched his hand to the ground in the required knuckling down position and shot his taw toward the other marbles. "Go," he whispered as the marble left his hand, and it did, striking a pretty yellow marble and knocking it out of the ring. His taw, though, was still inside the ring by quite a distance. He would get another shot, and his taw was in such a position as to hit another marble. It would take a strong shot.

"Again," Jack shouted. No one said a word as Jack leaned into the ring and took his aim. Jack's taw struck the marble, and rolled it out of the ring with the taw. He missed the next turn.

They're even now, thought Howard. Only two marbles were left in the ring, a green one and a yellow one. He leaned a little closer to the ring. If Bert hits with his first shot, he'll get another. Come on, hit it, he thought.

Bert took aim, and his black taw struck the green marble, sending it from the ring. Bert let go with a shout of joy. Howard looked quickly at Jack, who smiled, but Howard could see a look of fear in his brother's eyes. Jack hated so to lose. The other boys did not know how badly

Jack wanted to win this game, and Jack would never show it. Only Howard knew, and suddenly he could not hope for Bert's victory.

Bert stood and walked around the ring. He laughed, but it was a nervous laugh. Bert too wanted to win this game. "Let's have a little wager, Jack, me boy," he said.

"Don't know what we'd chance," said Jack, but his voice showed his interest.

"Have any food left in your haversack?" Bert asked.

"Just enough for supper tonight, some bread and bits of cheese and apples."

"I've some salt pork," said Bert. "Want to wager?"

"It's a deal," said Jack, and he smiled.

Bert knelt and took his aim. Howard knew that Jack held his breath. The taw left Bert's fingers, collided with the green marble, and knocked it from the ring.

"Good show!" shouted Roger. Bert jumped up, slapped Jack on the back, and began to do a bit of a jig. Howard wished he had not watched the game.

"All right, all right," said Jack, and he managed a smile. "You'll get my supper, but I get to keep five more marbles than I started the game with."

They were, of course, playing for keeps. Howard knew that his brother always played for keeps. He could not let it go at that, though. "You'll have supper, brother," he said. "You've been invited to eat with me at old Cyrus's place."

Bert laughed. "Leave it to Jack to win one way or another."

Howard wanted to get away from them all. Even though at one point he had wanted Jack to lose, he could hardly bear it when he did. He went back toward

Molly's empty stall. Jack followed him and leaned on the gate after Howard went in. "Is it true, then? Am I really invited to old Cyrus's?"

"Yes." Howard dug under the straw to find his blanket. "Think I'll wash this," he announced. "The sun's bright. It will dry before night."

"I thought Cyrus didn't want anyone around his granddaughters. Wonder why he changed his mind."

Howard shrugged his shoulders. "Who knows?" He moved out of the stall. "I'm going to draw a bucket of water to use for the blanket," he said.

Again Jack followed. "By gum!" he shouted. "I've got a splendid idea. We'll have our sling competition after supper, and the girls can watch. There will be time before dark."

Howard whirled around to face his brother. "That's a crazy idea," he said. "Why would the girls want to see us throwing rocks from a leather strap? Even if they did, Cyrus would never hear of it. They have chores after supper, and there's Laura's lesson."

This time it was Jack who shrugged "Who knows? Anyway, it won't hurt to ask. You might be surprised."

Howard had a bit of soap, and he rubbed it on his blanket. Pushing the blanket into the sudsy water, he fretted. What would it be like taking Jack into one of Cyrus's suppers? Old Cyrus grumbled about everything, and his daughter, Mistress Donaldson, passed the bowls of food with few words between. Only Laura and Gracie could be expected to talk, or would Jack charm the whole family of them? Jack might even perform a miracle and cause silent Sarah to break into chatter.

He emptied the soapy water and drew fresh from the

well. He pushed the blanket up and down again to rinse it. Jack was determined to have the stupid sling contest. Howard wondered if there was a way he could hit himself in the head with the rock from his own sling. If there was, he was sure to do it.

Gracie came to the barn to call them to supper. She was clearly excited. "I can stand on my head," she said as soon as she saw Jack.

"Well," said Jack. "I can, too. Let's both stand on our heads together," and there they were, upside down in the straw, both with their legs straight in the air, Gracie unconcerned with her pantalets.

"Come on you two. I'm hungry," said Howard, and he went through the door. Jack and Gracie caught up with him.

"It's best we be whist and mum about standing on our heads in front of Grandpa and Ma. They mostly think people should stand on their feet, especially ladies, which is what they want me to be."

"I'll never tell," said Jack, and Gracie reached out to slip her hand into his.

Howard remembered Gracie's saying she did not want to meet Jack. He noticed a sour taste in his mouth. One of Mistress Donaldson's biscuits would fix that. If there's one left, he thought. Jack may pile them all on his own plate.

At the house, Howard was first to reach the porch step, but Jack moved around him with Gracie to go in first. "Hello, Mistress Donaldson," he was saying as Howard came in. "I'm Jackson Gardner," he added with a bow, "but most folks call me Jack."

"Welcome to our cottage," Mistress Donaldson said,

"and to our humble supper." She turned to Laura, who carried a bowl of steaming beans to the table. "This be Laura." Laura nodded her head.

It was the next introduction that shocked Howard. Mistress Donaldon moved her hand to indicate Sarah, who stood slightly away from the table. "This is Sarah, who ain't able to hear what you say or to speak a greeting."

Howard felt amazed. Hadn't they kept Sarah's malady a secret from him for as long as possible? Now here was her mother talking about it openly to a total stranger. It was what happened next that astonished him even more. Jack turned and bowed to the girl, and Sarah—silent, unresponsive Sarah—smiled at him, a quick, full smile that lit her face like a lantern lights a dark room.

Just then old Cyrus came into the room. "Aye, our company be here. We should gather round while the food is hot."

While they ate, Jack talked. He told about life in their little village and about how he and Howard had left school to help support their mother. "It was no great shakes to me, school I mean, but I wish Howard could have stayed. Howard's a bit of a scholar, he is."

Cyrus shook his head. "Book learning isn't what gets a man on, not around the canal, anyway. It's being a hard worker and having good common sense." He reached for more bread. "That's what I always say."

Howard looked down at his plate. Jack and Cyrus made being interested in education sound foolish. He glanced up and across the table at Laura. She smiled at him. "Well," she said, "I'm special pleased that Howard took well to school, him teaching me my letters and lots of words the way he's done."

Old Cyrus grunted. "I've come to consider learning will do you no harm. Mayhap you can write letters and such for your husband once you're wed. You're getting close to fifteen and comely. Won't be long till suitors come knocking at the door. Your grandmother was sixteen when we married up."

Howard saw Laura blush, and before he looked down he saw from the corner of his eye that Jack was smiling. He put down his fork, leaving part of a biscuit and a potato on his plate.

Jack began then to tell about his new sling, how he had worked for it, and how he had now taught his brother to use it also. "The sling is no easy thing to master," he said, "but Howard is good." He grinned widely. "Might be he's as good as me. We're going to find out this evening. Some of the hoggees down to the barn are fair excited about the competition." He turned to look at Cyrus. "The notion comes to me, sir, that you might want to come and watch, or maybe the young ladies."

"Oh, yes, Grandpa," said Gracie. "Can we?"

Howard swallowed hard, hoping Cyrus would be his old, cranky self, but the prospect of catching Jack for a grandson-in-law seemed to have cheered him considerably. "Always make it my practice to go to bed soon as supper's done, but it's no matter to me if the girls want to watch you sling the thing." He nodded toward Sarah. "I'd not want Sarie put in harm's way. She's to be kept away from them other boys, you hear me, Laura? You stay right beside her."

"There's your lesson to consider, Laura," Howard said.

"Well," she said, smiling, "you can't very well teach

me and compete with Jack at the same time. Guess I've had my last lesson. I'm on my own now."

All five of the other hoggees waited just over the hill that separated Cyrus's house from the barn. "Here they come now," one of the boys yelled when the group appeared at the top of the hill, "and I'll be hanged if they ain't got girls with them!"

Gracie giggled, and Laura, who already held Sarah's hand, also took Gracie's. "We'll watch from here," she said.

"I'll tell them to leave you be," said Jack, and he went off to speak to the other boys.

Howard stood quietly, leaning his weight first on one foot and then the other until Jack looked back at him and called, "Come on down here."

Howard turned to the girls. "Well, then, I suspect you'll be going back to the house as soon as the competition is over. Tomorrow it's the canal for us bright and early." He shifted his weight again. "Work hard at the lessons, Laura."

"Oh, I will, Howard. I will." She stepped toward him, and Howard thought she was about to say something more.

Suddenly though, Jack was back, and the girls turned toward him. "I wanted to tell you good-bye," he said, and he bowed to the girls. "I'm so glad I got the chance to meet you."

"Good-bye, Jack," Laura said.

Howard spun around to run down the hill. "Good luck to you, Howard," Laura called. "Good luck in the contest and on the canal."

Howard glanced over his shoulder at her, but she was talking now to Jack. There was, he decided, no use to call back to her, not while she talked to Jack. There was no use to think about Laura at all, not if Jack took a fancy to her. At the bottom of the hill, he waited for his brother with eyes down.

Jack had a big bucket for a target turned over the fence post in front of the barn. "You want to go first or me?" he asked when he joined Howard.

Howard bit at his lip, thinking. He might as well get it over with. "I'll go first," he said.

Jack turned to the audience and held up his arms to make an announcement. "We'll shoot three rounds," he called, making his voice loud enough for the girls to hear him. "May the best man win." He handed the sling and three rocks to Howard.

Howard put two of the rocks in his pocket, loaded the strap, and began to whirl it above his head, keeping his eye on the target. Let her fly, he told himself, and the rock hit the bucket sending a big thump into the air.

Howard heard Laura yell, "Good shot!"

Jack called, "That a boy! Now go at it again."

Howard took the strap and whirled it again. This time he missed, and he heard Laura's "Oh!"

"Give it another go," said Jack. "You've still got a chance to win."

Howard loaded his last rock. Good old Jack. He always wanted there to be a possibility that Howard might actually beat him. What fun would it be to beat someone who had no chance? He began to twirl the sling. Take your time, he told himself. When he was certain his aim was good, he let go.

It seemed to Howard that the rock was in the air a very long time. He could watch no longer and had just dropped his gaze when he heard the wonderful thump.

"Two out of three," one of the boys shouted, and Howard heard Laura clap.

Howard handed the sling off to Bert, who took it to Jack. For an instant, Howard thought of going to stand beside the girls, but he decided not to. He had already said his good-bye. He walked toward the group of boys but stopped a bit away from them.

Bert came to stand beside him while Jack loaded his first rock. "The fellows are mostly pulling for you," he said. "They don't like to say it right out on account of Jack being everybody's mate, but they're pulling for you, them all having been beat by him in some kind of game."

"Everyone feels for the underdog, I suppose," said Howard, and he pushed his hands into his trouser pockets. He wondered if Laura liked the underdog, and he wondered if Laura knew her grandfather had hopes of marrying her off to Jack. He thought the idea should not seem so revolting to him. Howard certainly had no desire to marry anyone, not even a remote desire. So why should he care if Cyrus happened to be successful in his plan?

Jack, of course, never missed a shot. Howard knew he wouldn't. He even found himself half hoping Jack wouldn't miss. He was not used to winning. When his opponent was his brother, it felt more comfortable to lose. He heard Laura cheering for Jack, just as she had cheered for him, and the sound made him angry.

That night in the barn, Howard waited until he was certain the others boys were asleep. Taking his board, he slipped through the small opening he had deliberately left in the barn door. Pushing the heavy door open would have caused too much noise. Howard did not want company.

The moon was full and bright. He climbed the slight hill to the spot where the girls had stood watching the contest. Settling himself on the grass, he took his knife from his pocket, then sat soaking in the scene. Tomorrow he would leave the spot where he had survived the winter. Before him was the barn that now seemed like home. He turned his head and shoulders to look at Cyrus's house, where the family slept, the others as silent now as Sarah.

He wanted to write about it all on his board, but he knew he had neither time nor space to carve the full story of his winter.

He sat for a long time on the hill remembering his friendship with the girls, the supper with Jack at Cyrus's house, and the sling competition. When the dampness of the early spring night began to chill his bones, he took his knife and carved the familiar words about Jack winning.

# 8

## THERE IS A BOOK
## FOR SARAH

It did not take Howard long on the canal to make the magnificent discovery, and he carved the words with excitement. That next morning after the contest all seven boys had been up before dawn. "It's back to work for us," Howard told Molly, and he brushed her before he put the bright, new blue harness on her. Bert took care of Molly's working partner, Lillie. Just before daylight the boys fastened the two mules together. "Gee up!" Howard called when they were out of the barn, even though he knew the mules would turn right without his direction.

Howard's team was first to leave the barn, but the other boys and mules were right behind them. Jack, as befitting his new position, had gone down to the dock early. Just as the sun became visible, Howard saw the boats.

Captain Travis was there to board *The Red Bird* and to see his other two boats off for the first trip of the season. Captain Wall, a man for whom Howard had never worked, would be in charge of *The Blue Bird* this season. The boats were lined up along the dock. Their blue, red, and yellow colors had been repainted. "They're pretty, ain't they?" said Bert, and Howard agreed. "I hope I can work up, same as Jack done," said Bert. "It would be a grand thing to be a captain under Captain Travis."

Howard grunted. He knew that they were lucky to work for Captain Travis, who, unlike some of the captains, made sure his mules and his boys were well fed and not pushed too far. Mules were changed at stations every ten miles. Boys worked six hours on and six hours off. It was hard work, but some boys and mules were pushed harder, worked until they grew lame or fell on the path. Still, Howard didn't want to work forever on the canal.

"Hoisting the tow! Look sharp!" Jack called from the boat. Howard and Bert hurried to get the rope and fasten it securely to the doubletree, the bar to which the mules' harnesses had been connected.

Jack was a crew member now, and he wore a blue jacket and a blue cap with a bill. As bowman, his job was to keep the towrope clear of debris on the canal, check it always for strain, and to fasten it when the boat docked or went into a lock.

Howard looked at his brother in uniform. He would not be sleeping in the back hall now, where the hoggees' bunks folded down from the wall outside the crew's small room. The bowman, helmsman, and cook slept in a tiny room unless the cook happened to be a woman, who would then sleep in her kitchen.

"All right if I take the first call?" asked Bert.

Howard nodded. "Guess I'll say good-bye to Molly." He went to the mule and patted her shoulder. "You'll be in Albany resting up before I'm on the towpath." It was the same with each first day. Captain Travis's boats wintered in Birchport, as did all his mules. Some mules went ahead on flatboats. All three of the packet boats went first to Albany, ten miles away, where they got fresh mules and headed back up the canal toward Buffalo.

Howard would encounter Molly again on the trip, but he did not know where or when. "Bye, old girl," he whispered to the mule. "Thanks for sharing your stall with me all winter." Suddenly he was desperately afraid tears might come to his eyes. He was to be separated from Molly, and in a way from Jack. He shook his head and called out the canal boy's friendly insult. "Hey, Bert, don't drown in the canal." He turned and boarded the boat. He supposed he should warn himself. If anyone could drown in the four feet of canal water, he could.

The new cook was indeed a woman. Howard saw her at the stove as he passed the kitchen door. Maybe I should go in and welcome her to *The Blue Bird*, he thought, and he stepped back to stand in the door.

"Hello," he said. "My name's Howard."

The tall, dark woman looked up from the potato she had been slicing into a bowl. "Don't care what your name is," she said flatly. "Captain says you eat all you want, but I don't talk to you. Della no like boys."

Howard moved on down the hall. He wondered if the cook talked so rudely to everyone. Maybe she was a marvelous cook, and Captain Travis did not care about her manners. Maybe Howard had found his future. Maybe he would become a top-notch cook and talk to people as he pleased. He smiled at the far-fetched idea. He knew he should spend his six hours off resting, but he was not tired. He'd go up to the deck on top of the cabin. There were no interesting passengers to watch here at Birchport, but there would be at Albany.

He had just settled himself on the deck when Captain Wall blew the whistle, and *The Blue Bird* pulled away from the dock. Howard turned from where he was looking off to one side and looked back at the dock. What he saw there really surprised him. Three girls stood on the dock. It took a minute for him to realize that Sarah, Laura, and Gracie were really there. He leaned over the deck and was about to yell good-bye when he realized they were waving toward the bow, where Jack was.

Howard moved to the other end of the deck and looked down at the bow of the boat, where Jack stood waving his cap at the girls. "Where's Howard?" he heard Laura call, but by then the boat was pulling away. Howard did not wave or call. He doubted Laura would really want to see him, not with Jack in his handsome uniform to look at. He turned and walked slowly back to the other end of the deck.

Howard knew the packet boats moved at about four miles an hour. It would take two and a half hours to get to Albany, where the mules would be changed and passengers would board before the boat turned back to go up the canal to Buffalo. He started to sit back down on the deck bench, but suddenly he did feel tired. It would be best, he decided, if he went to his bunk to rest while the boat was quiet.

He moved down the back stairs. He was glad he did not have to go through the kitchen to get to the back hall and his fold-down bunk. He took his pillow from a small footlocker where he had stored his haversack, let down the lower board bed, and climbed onto it. The boat moved smoothly down the calm canal. Howard listened to the sound of the lapping water. When he dreamed, he dreamed of the fire.

The boat stopped, and Howard woke. He wanted to see the passengers load at Albany. The boat, when full, could hold as many as forty-five people, but there would not be that many on this trip, so early in the season. Still, Howard did not want to miss them. Some poorer people rode the line boat that also carried goods. Packets like *The Blue Bird* were only for travelers, and he always enjoyed watching them.

He went down to the bow of the boat. Jack climbed onto the dock, took the great rope from the mules' harnesses, and fastened it to the dock. Next Jack moved to help the passengers step aboard. Many of the travelers were men, some dressed in suits for business. There were women, too, with bright hats and parasols.

Two women traveled with a child, a girl of about ten. She carried a huge yellow cat, and the older of the two women carried a sort of boxed cage that Howard knew must be meant to keep the cat from running about the boat.

Howard watched Jack reach for the cat, thinking he would hold it while the girl boarded the boat. The girl turned away from him. "My granddaughter never allows strangers to hold Matilda," the older woman said, "but if you would be so kind as to take this carrier, I would appreciate it."

"Yes, ma'am," Jack said, and he took the carrier from the woman and followed her across the boat. Howard knew Jack would likely earn a handsome tip from the woman, who was extremely well dressed.

Just before it was time for his shift to begin, Howard went into the dining room to fill his plate. Hoggees did not eat with passengers as the rest of the crew did. They took their food back to the sleeping hall to eat. Food was one of the good things about being a hoggee, at least on Captain Travis's boats. Two long tables were filled with food—bread, cheese, ham, a pork roast, mashed potatoes, gravy, sweet potatoes, corn, two kinds of beans, two kinds of cake, and three kinds of pie.

Howard filled his plate, leaving just enough room for dessert. He was adding a piece of chocolate cake when he saw the cat people again. This time the cat rode in the carrier, carried by the younger of the two women. "I'll put Matilda over there, Mother," she said, and she nodded toward a bench beside a window. "You and Susan go ahead and begin to get your food." She started to move toward the bench, but the girl reached out and pulled at her dress.

The woman turned to the child, who held up her hands and moved her fingers. The mother set the cat carrier down, and she, too, began to move her hands. Howard watched the girl nod. The woman made one more movement with her fingers, nodded herself, then lifted the carrier and moved to put it beneath the bench.

Howard's heart began to beat fast. What were Susan and her mother doing? He stood by the door and watched as the women and the girl filled their plates. "Does Susan like cherry pie?" the grandmother asked the mother when she joined them at the dessert table.

"Give her apple," the mother answered. Howard noticed that Susan said nothing. He wanted to watch these people more, wanted to sit near them. What if the new cook caught him eating with the passengers? Would that mean trouble with Captain Wall? He looked toward the kitchen behind the dining room. The cook was back there, unlikely to come out with more food at least for a while.

Howard decided to risk the cook's wrath. The little girl and her mother sat on one side of the table. The grandmother was across from them. Only four other people had come into the dining room. Holding his breath, Howard moved to a space just down from the grandmother. Her large cloth bag was on the bench between them.

While he ate, he watched and listened. The women discussed how the dining room would become the sleeping area at night. "See that big red curtain," said the older woman, nodding toward a curtain gathered at the end of the room. "They pull it out to separate the women from the men. We've been assigned that first bench to sleep on. They will put pads on it. Some people will sleep on those shelves that get folded down from the wall."

The younger woman turned to the girl beside her, and moved her fingers. The girl turned to look at the curtain and the shelves. Her mother's telling her about how they will sleep, Howard thought. She's talking to her with her hands!

"How do you say *bed?*" the grandmother asked, but before her daughter could answer, the woman went on. "No, don't tell me. I want to look it up. I'll remember better if I look it up for myself." She reached into the bag and pulled out a large book. She began to turn through the pages.

In amazement, Howard leaned closer to the grandmother. Forgetting his shyness, he touched the woman's arm. "Is the little girl deaf and mute?" he asked.

The woman turned to answer him, but just then the cook came barreling from the kitchen. She was even taller than Howard had realized, and big-boned. Her thick, dark hair was pulled back from a high forehead. The sleeves on her dress were very short, and she waved her long, dark arms as she stormed into the dining room. "Hoggee out!" she shouted. "No hoggees in dining room! Shoo!" She grabbed the bottom corners of her apron and began to flap it up and down.

Howard scrabbled up from the bench, hitting his knee on the table. "He bother you?" he heard the cook ask the women, but she did not wait for an answer. "Hoggees dirty and thieving. Steal and stink!"

For a minute Howard stood frozen. He did not want to leave without a look at that book, and he had to ask some questions. The table was between him and the cook, but she reached out as if to snatch him and drag him across to her side. Howard backed up out of her reach.

Everyone in the dining room stared at him. He bent toward the grandmother. "Madam," he said to the grandmother, "please, I need to . . ." He cut his words off. The cook was going to the end of the table to come around to his side.

"Rascal!" she yelled. "You filthy scamp!"

Howard ran. At the doorway, he looked over his shoulder. The cook had stopped pursuing him. She leaned heavily on the table beside the grandmother, and she talked, her words pouring out too quickly for Howard to understand them from a distance.

He moved through the door and up the steps to the deck on top of the main cabin. He knew it must be almost time for him to take Bert's place on the towpath. The captain was sure to check to see that the change had been made. The deck was full of people enjoying one of the first really springlike days. Howard made his way through the people. He noticed a young couple whose hands were locked together and who stared into each other's eyes. They did not look at him as he pushed his way around them.

Near the front stairs, three gentlemen stood smoking large cigars. He looked behind him. The cook did not seem to be chasing him. "Excuse me," he said to the smokers, and he ducked between them to go downstairs.

At his bunk, he took his haversack from the footlocker. There would be just enough time to record his exciting discovery. His heart beat fast as he carved. He did not care that he had been chased and screamed at. Nothing mattered but seeing that miraculous book. He carved quickly, then, smiling, went out.

Jack was on duty at the front of the boat, but Howard did not go over to him. He knew if he did, he would end up telling Jack what had happened. He did not want his brother to know he was already in trouble. He also did not want to tell him what he had just learned about deaf people; not yet.

Howard went quickly to the boat's edge and looked at the bank of the canal. He would like to be able to jump instead of asking the helmsman to steer the boat closer to the side. It would be better if he did nothing at this point to call attention to himself. Could he make it? Once last year, he had tried too big a jump and had ended up in the canal. Remembering, he made a face. The fall had been late in the season, not while the water was fresh from Lake Erie. Howard had fallen into water full of coal silt dumped from stoves, sewage from the toilets, and all sorts of debris thrown into the canal by travelers.

He looked again at the distance from the towpath. Yes, he could make it. He walked back as far as he could go, took a running jump, and landed on the path. Bert walked ahead of him behind the mules. Howard called out to him. "Time for me to take over," and he ran to catch up.

"Captain Travis bought some new mules. These are named Carl and Fred." He patted the larger mule. "Carl here's a good fellow, but Fred bears watching."

"Thanks," said Howard, and he took the reins.

Bert stepped aside and bent to rub his legs. "Out of practice," he said. "I'll have to ask Captain Wall for some liniment." He limped toward the boat.

"The new cook's a wild woman. Chased me out of the dining room. Be careful."

"Don't drown in the canal," Bert called. Then he yelled to the helmsman, "Bring her over for me, please, Mister Buck. I've done in my legs with walking."

Howard felt safe now. No one would interfere with the mule driver on the towpath. Hoggees were the lowliest worker on the canal, but in a way they were also the most important. Someone had to keep the mules on the path. Someone had to urge them along.

Without the mules, the boats did not move. Sometimes when captains of packet boats decided to race, hoggees would climb on the mules because they couldn't keep up when the mules ran. Four miles an hour was the canal speed limit because fast boats were likely to hit the sides and cause damage to the banks. Captains who raced had to pay a fine of ten dollars, but races still happened, especially later in the season when everyone was tired and looking for a diversion.

Howard made his own diversion, and he kept it secret. He sang to the mules. Keeping his voice low so only the animals could hear, he sang all the songs he knew: "America," "Old Dan Tucker," "Amazing Grace," "Buffalo Girls." When he grew tired of repeating songs, he started making up new words to old tunes. Once he had actually written down words he made up to go with the tune from "Old Kentucky Home." It was all about the stars that saw what went on below them on the Erie Canal.

Now, though, there was no singing. Howard had to think. He went back over what he had seen in the dining room. The little girl had never said a word, nor had her grandmother or mother spoken to her. She was deaf and mute, just like Sarah. Howard was certain of the fact. There was, however, one big difference. The little girl's mother talked to her with her hands, not just pointing to tasks the girl should do. Howard remembered how she had turned to the girl to explain the curtain. The girl talked back too.

A thrill passed through his body, leaving his arms covered with goose bumps. No, this Susan was not like Sarah, not really. He looked back over his shoulder at the boat. The little girl on that boat was not like Sarah at all. She was not locked in a prison of silence.

"Fellows," he said to the mules, "I've got something to tell you. There's this girl I know. She's a real nice girl, but she's sad, so awful sad because she can't ever talk to her sisters or know what is said at the supper table." He put the reins over his shoulder, reached out both hands, and patted the mules on their sides. "We might be able to help her, but I need to see that book."

He had to plan. The *clip-clop* of mules' hooves on the towpath filled his ears and eased his mind so that he could think. His shift would be over at six o'clock in the evening. Supper would be mostly over, especially with so small a passenger load. He would not go into the dining room to fill his plate. He had hardly eaten anything at noon, and his stomach was empty. No, it did not matter. Hadn't he been hungry plenty of times during the winter? He would not risk stirring up the cook by going into her domain, not tonight.

Probably he would find the family on the deck. The evening would be warm, and the lights of the boats and the stars above made a pretty sight. From the way the grandmother described the curtain, he knew the younger woman and the girl had not been on a packet boat before. The captains blew the whistles more at night, too, and the atmosphere on the cabin-top deck was like a party, often with a musician. Yes, he was certain to find the family on the deck.

Suddenly, Howard's mind was jerked back to his job. A bridge loomed in front of him, and Jack's voice was calling, "Low bridge, everybody down." Howard's hands shook as he removed the reins from his shoulders. It was the hoggee's job to call out about the bridge. Then the bowman took up the call, warning the passengers who were on the high deck.

If Jack had not been looking, no one would have warned the passengers. People could be knocked down by the low bridges. They could be injured or even killed. Howard gave himself a shaking. Yes, it was good to plan how he would help Sarah, but he had to be careful about his job, too. Frequently they passed under bridges built over the canal because farmers had their land split by the water and had to be able to reach the other side. Bridges were low, too, because high bridges were expensive to build.

"Look smart, Howard," Jack called. "Get your mind on your business."

Howard's face turned red. He had barely started the job, had walked only a few miles, and already the bow-man had found it necessary to warn him. Howard bit at his lip. He had to do better. The scolding hurt more because the bowman was his brother, his brother in a grown-up uniform doing a grown-up job. He had messed up twice already on his first day back at work. He had to do better!

He kept his eyes on the path ahead. "Low bridge," he called out as soon as the next structure came into view, and he felt better.

"Low bridge, everybody down," Jack called. Howard wondered if the mother would sign the message to the little girl or if she would push her down and explain later. He knew that the child would be told about the bridges and the farmers who had to cross them to tend to their fields. Whatever was in that book, the one in the grandmother's bag, it had set Susan free from silence.

Howard's legs, like Bert's, ached by the time his shift was over. "Captain will give you the liniment," Bert told him when he took the reins. "It fixed me right well."

Howard did not have time for liniment. He did not know where the family might get off the boat. He had to talk to them tonight. He sat down for a moment on the tiny lower deck, reached down to rub his legs, and gave himself another talking to. Just walk by the dining room, he told himself, look in to see if they're eating. If they are, go up and wait for them. No, why not just go directly to the deck? It was not against the rules for him to go into the dining room to fill his plate, but it would be better to take no chances. The cook might still yell at him about his earlier mistake.

He climbed the front steps. The deck had several people on it, some standing about in small groups, some seated on chairs and benches. He looked them over and smiled when he saw them. Susan, with her cat in her arms, sat with her mother and grandmother on a bench at the other end of the deck. His eyes searched for the bag. There it was under the bench beside the empty cat box.

Biting his lip, he made his way through the people. He had just about reached them when the older woman looked up and saw him. "Stop where you are, young man," she said loudly. "I don't want you to come any closer. We've been warned about boys like you! Now get away!"

Howard stopped. He could feel the eyes of the crowd on him. A large man who sat not far from the woman stood up. "Are you deaf, boy?" he shouted. "The lady does not want to talk to you. Now get away before I teach you some manners!"

Howard ran! He ran back through the crowd, down the stairs, and back to his bunk.

On his own bunk he felt safe. No one could fault him for being in his own bed. He lay, his heart pounding and his body shaking against the hard wood. What could he do? He knew the cook had turned the women against him. It was true that some of the boys who worked on the canal were rough. Many of them were orphans who had never been taught how to behave. They were homeless and survived the winter the best they could, just as he had done, but he had not turned to stealing. It was unfair for him to be judged by other boys' behavior. He sighed. Things weren't always fair. Was it fair for Sarah to be deaf?

Should he go to Jack for help? No, Jack would say that Howard should mind his own business, to look sharp. He would say that old Cyrus would not want to know about the book, anyway. Howard clenched his fists. He had to see that book!

He was calmer now, no more shaking body or racing heart. A plan began to form in his mind. He would have to sneak a look at the book. Hadn't the mother said they had been assigned the first bench for sleeping? Yes, he was sure of that. He could slip into the ladies' side of the cabin at night, take the book from the bag, carry it out to the hallway, where a lantern would allow him to read it. When he was satisfied, he would slip back into the cabin and replace the book. He could do that, couldn't he? "Yes," he said aloud. "I can."

His next shift would begin at twelve. The process of bedding down began at nine. Most people would be asleep by ten. No, he would wait until ten thirty to be certain. The bench was right by the door. He would not have to go far, and it would be dark. No one was likely to see him.

Time went by slowly. Finally darkness fell and lanterns were lit. When Jack and the helmsman came by to sleep while the night crew took over, Howard held his breath and lay very still. Only when they had passed into the tiny room where the crew slept did he breathe again.

From the main cabin he could hear the preparations

for changing the dining hall into a sleeping room. The folding beds made a creaking noise as they were let down. Howard had never noticed before how much noise went into making the beds. Pads were spread on benches and tables, and people talked and laughed. Someone coughed over and over. On other trips he had slept through it all. Now he wondered how.

Finally, the cabin grew quieter. The snoring started. Some snored softly and could only be heard between the loud snorts of their neighbors. Howard hoped Susan, her mother, and grandmother were able to sleep through so much racket.

A big clock hung on the wall, and Howard watched it. The hands moved slowly toward ten thirty. When finally the time had come, he eased himself off the bunk. There was no need for tiptoeing until he got into the main cabin, but he stepped lightly, anyway, almost afraid to breathe.

Now he was in the main hall. The door to the cabin was slightly ajar. Howard's hand shook as he reached for the knob. Very slowly he eased open the door, just enough to squeeze through. For a moment he stood looking in. No, it would be better if he crawled into the room.

He dropped to all fours and eased his body through the opening. There was too much light from the hall. He reached back and pushed the door almost closed. For a moment he stayed perfectly still, letting his eyes grow accustomed to the blackness. Then he began to make out tables and benches with dark shapes on them. The walls were full of fold-down bunks like his except these were covered with pads for comfort. He inched into the room. The first bench was right before him, and there was the bag beneath the bench. Slowly he moved his hands and knees toward the bench. When he could touch the bag, he drew in a deep breath and reached for it.

The bag felt heavy, and he tugged at it. It slid slightly away from the bench. Howard reached for the sides. He pulled them apart, and put his shaking hand inside. First he touched an object made of cloth, probably a scarf. He pushed it aside, and his fingers touched the book. He had it! Carefully he began to draw it out of the bag. Just then the cat, still in the box, let out a loud, long *meow* as if it had been attacked!

"Matilda," the grandmother said softly, and she dropped her hand from her bed. The hand brushed her bag, and she sat up, screaming. "Help! Help! I'm being robbed!"

Howard sprang to his feet and turned back to the door. He ran for the stairs. He could hear someone behind him, but he did not look over his shoulder. Racing for the steps, he flung his body onto the first step. He had made it to step four when he felt the hand around his ankle. "Got you, you little devil," a man's voice said, and the strength went out of Howard's body.

# 9

# SOME PEOPLE ARE
# WONDERFULLY KIND

The great, unexpected kindness overwhelmed Howard. After he carved the words, he was surprised to feel tears slipping from his eyes. He had never before cried with joy. But before that wonderful moment, there were dark ones.

They stood in the captain's small cabin. Howard had been dragged there by the man who caught him on the stairs. He sat now in a small wooden chair, his face in his hands.

The grandmother was there, too, along with the captain, a large, red-faced man. Jack had come in just as the captain shoved Howard into the chair. Howard did not know how Jack had learned of his predicament. He also did not know whether he was glad his brother stood in a line with those who accused him, or whether he wished they had thrown him overboard with weights around his feet so that he could have drowned peacefully in the canal without his brother ever having to know what had happened.

"By thunder," bellowed Captain Wall, "I'll throw you off the boat tonight, with no town near. I won't tolerate a thieving hoggee! I won't."

Jack moved around the grandmother to speak to the captain. "Please, sir," he said softly, "if I might say a word in my brother's defense." The captain nodded slightly, and Jack rushed on. "My brother, sir, is no thief. I can't tell you what he was doing with that bag, but sir, I would wager my life on the fact that he was not stealing. Let him explain please, sir."

An angry huff came from the woman. "His hand was in my bag. I saw that with my own eyes!"

Howard raised his head then. "Please, madam," he said, and his voice shook. "I wanted to see the book, the one about how to talk with your hands."

"Are you daft, boy?" said the captain. "Talk with your hands. What gibberish is that?"

"For deaf people, sir. This lady has a book that shows how to talk to deaf people." Howard looked pleadingly at the lady.

The woman looked at Howard long and hard before she spoke. "It's true, Captain," she said. "My granddaughter is a deaf-mute, and we have a book that shows how to communicate with her."

The captain reached out, grabbed the collar of Howard's shirt, and pulled him roughly to his feet. "And why," he thundered, "would the likes of you be wanting a book. You can't read, can you, boy?"

"I can, sir," said Howard, "and I wanted to see the book for a friend, a friend who cannot hear or speak."

The captain shoved the boy back into the chair. "That's a likely story." The captain shook his large head, and the red in his face deepened. "If you had an honest desire, why did you not speak to the lady? Why did you not ask?"

"I tried, sir," said Howard, and a small hope flamed in his heart.

The woman sighed. "It's true," she said. "The boy tried to speak to me, but the cook said I should not trust him. She said his kind is up to no good."

"Our cook, madam, has an excellent hand in the kitchen. She may not prove to be so good a character judge as she is a judge of a good recipe." Then he turned back to Howard. This time he put his hand on the boy's shoulder. "God help me, boy, I believe you. If I find you to be false later, God will not be able to help you. But if not a thief, you are at least a fool to go pawing about in the ladies' sleeping chamber. Many a captain on this canal would have drowned you for such an act without giving you so much as a word in your own defense."

"You are a generous and patient man, sir," said Jack quickly, "and a fair one, too. My brother and I are grateful, aren't we, Howard?" He shot Howard a look that meant speak.

"Yes," said Howard. "Oh, yes, very grateful!"

"Save your gratitude," said the captain. "I am not finished with you yet." He turned to the woman. "Madam," he said, "this boy is due back on the towpath. To punish him now would also be to punish the other hoggee who waits for relief."

The woman's face softened. "He need not be punished at all, sir, as far as I am concerned."

The captain shook his head. "No, my dear lady, this boy disturbed your sleep and the sleep of many other passengers. I cannot take such behavior lightly." He took his hand from Howard's shoulder. "When you are next off duty, you will report to the cook. I daresay she can think of a way to keep you busy for a few hours. Now get out on the towpath, boy, and mind you, the next time you get yourself into trouble, you will not find me so lenient."

For the next six hours, Howard walked behind the mules, Joe and Otis. They were a docile pair, well accustomed to the towpath. Every inch of his body ached from lack of sleep, and his head felt strange, as if he walked in a dream. "I'll sing," he told the mules after a time, and for a while the songs eased his weariness. Then his mind became too tired, and he could not think of the words.

Somehow, he made it until six in the morning. "Hey," said Bert when he came to take over. "I've heard some wild stories about you, I have! Old Howard in the ladies' sleeping chamber! Now that's one for you! Who would have thought the likes of you would be up to such shenanigans." He reached out and slapped Howard on the back.

"If I had the strength, I'd wallop you one," said Howard, but he grinned. He turned and went back to the boat, glad to see that it almost touched the canal bank on his side. The helmsman was likely asleep. At least the jump back on would be all right.

He gathered what seemed to be his last bit of energy and jumped onto the boat. Now he had to face the cook. He pulled himself up as straight as he could and made his way toward the kitchen. He found the kitchen door closed, and he paused outside of it. Was it possible that the cook was still in bed? Breakfast, he knew, was not served until eight so passengers need not be awakened too early. The meal had to be prepared, but maybe she could do that while the captain oversaw the storing of mattress pads. He leaned close to the door to listen. There was no sound. Suddenly, however, he felt a heavy hand grab his shoulder. He swung around to face the cook.

"I was listening to see if you were still asleep," he said quickly. "I didn't want to wake you."

"At this hour? Still asleep?" She made a snorting sound. "There'd be no breakfast on this boat then!" She let him go.

"The captain said I should help you." He leaned back against the wall as far from her as possible.

She, too, leaned, extending her long neck so that her face was not far from his. "You look puny," she said. "Been working all night, right?"

He nodded. She waved her arms. "Go away. You come back some other day to help Della."

Amazed, Howard inched away from the wall. "Thank you," he said. "I will. I promise to come back to help you."

The big woman nodded her head. "I think maybe I was wrong about you," she said. "I think maybe not all hoggees steal."

"Thank you," Howard said again, and moved away down the hall toward his bunk, too tired to think. When his sleep was disturbed five hours later by the laughter of some passengers who walked by his hall, he sprang up. He had not meant to sleep so long. He had to find the woman with the book. Surely she would talk to him now.

He hurried through the main cabin, but there was no sign of the family. He climbed the stairs to the deck, his eyes scanning the group even before his feet reached the top. No sign of Susan, her mother, or her grandmother.

The boat was not big. A great fear began to grow inside him. Jack sat at the front of the boat on duty as the bowman.

"Have you seen the deaf girl?" Howard called before he reached his brother.

"They got off," said Jack, "a couple of hours ago at Schenectady."

"What? You let them go without telling me!" Howard drew in his breath and let it go in an explosion. "You knew I wanted to see that book."

"The captain helped them off. I didn't want to bring up the book in front of him." Jack shook his head. "We got to keep these jobs, brother."

Howard turned away. He did not want to talk more to Jack. He did not want to talk to anyone. Later, on the towpath, he was able to talk to the mules, Annie and Betty. "I won't give up," he said. "I will find a way to help Sarah. I will."

When his shift was finished, he went into the dining room to fill his plate for the evening meal. He had just finished covering a large slice of beef with gravy when a voice called, "Hoggee, I look for you."

The cook came toward him from the kitchen. For a second, Howard considered dropping the gravy ladle and bolting from the room, but the woman looked friendly. When he saw what was in her hand, he pulled in his breath with surprise.

She pushed the large brown book toward him. "Here," she said. "The lady leave this with Della, she say give it to the hoggee."

"Oh," he said, "the hand-talking book." He set down his plate to take the book. A piece of paper stuck out from under the cover. Howard pulled it out and read:

*Dear Young Man,*
*I want you to have this book. I can get another. My*
*granddaughter has been to a special school for the deaf in*
*New York City. We are headed home now. I wish you*
*well and hope the book helps your friend.*
                                              *Sincerely,*
                                    *Mrs. John L. Brewer*

"She gave it to me. She gave me the book," Howard
said, half to the cook and half to himself.

The woman smiled. "You tell Della what book say.
You tell me when you come to help."

"Tomorrow," said Howard. He grabbed up his plate,
and with the book under his arm he headed back to his
bunk.

While he ate, he read. There was, he learned, a finger
movement used as a sign for each letter in the alphabet,
but that wouldn't help Sarah, who couldn't read. There
were movements, though, for words. Howard remembered that Mrs. Brewer had wondered how to say *bed.*
He looked up the word. Then, following the instruc-
tions, he tilted his head to the side to rest on his open
hand. Next, he used his index finger to indicate first the
front legs of a bed and then the back legs. He practiced
the sign again.

Howard flipped through the book. He could learn
the signs and teach them to Sarah and Laura. The girls
would be able to talk to each other.

When his meal was finished, he took one of the small
boards from his haversack and carved. With each letter
he felt gratitude to the woman, Mrs. Brewer. He would
study the book, learn the signs, and find a way to teach
Sarah when winter came.

For six weeks, Howard walked the towpath. His legs no longer ached so badly at the end of his turn. Every day he studied the book and practiced sign language. Some days he spent time in the kitchen with the cook. Della did not talk to any of the other crew members, but now Howard was her friend. He told her about the girls, and he even taught her the sign for cook, the action of turning over a pancake. Sometimes they would make the sign to each other across the dining room when Howard came in to fill his plate.

He sat on a stool in Della's kitchen one day, helping her peel potatoes. She moved from the stove to the window. "We at that Birchport right now," she said, and Howard felt the boat stop. He went to stand beside Della and look out. Bert was leading the mules away to be exchanged for rested ones, and some passengers were waiting to board.

Howard looked up the hill. He could not see the barn or Cyrus's house from the canal, but he knew they were there, just a short walk away.

Della seemed to read his thoughts. "Why you not get off?" she asked. "Why you not go teach some signs to girls?"

Howard walked back to the stool, took up his knife, and began to peel again. "I have to earn money for my mother," he said, "and besides, I'm not sure Cyrus would let me teach Sarah. I'd have no place to stay either." He shook his head. "It isn't as easy as just getting off the boat."

"*Humph!*" She threw up her hands in exasperation. "If Della give up so quick, she not be cooking on *Blue Bird*. She be back on the island looking for some poor husband to support."

Work schedules left little time to spend with Jack, but Howard did not mind. He had a purpose now, a driving force that had nothing to do with his brother. Just once he talked about the book to Jack. They were sharing a meal, and his brother did not even look up from his food. "There's nothing for it but to give the book to Laura when we close down for the winter. Maybe she can read enough now to help Sarah. There's no use you studying all that stuff."

"There is a reason," he said firmly, and he did study. He ached to share his knowledge. Then at the end of April, something happened. The boat's rudder snapped.

"Christopher Columbus!" called the helmsman. "I can't steer her without a rudder."

"Stop the mules," Jack called, and Howard stopped them.

Captain Wall came to the bow, and after some deliberation it was decided that they should go slowly on to Birchport, only twenty miles away. They were returning from Buffalo, and only the passengers bound for Albany would not have been delivered. "We'll have to lay over there for repairs," said the captain. "Thank God this run is almost done. Our passengers will continue on other boats."

Howard went back to his mules. He slowed the pace of the mules' hooves, but the pace of his mind picked up. He would be in Birchport for a day, maybe two. He would sleep in Cyrus's barn. Would there be work for him to do on the boat? Surely, there would be a chance to see Laura and Sarah. This was his chance to show them the book. His heart raced.

Jack left the bow and came out to walk beside Howard. "Do you know what tomorrow is?" he asked.

Howard shrugged, "Saturday, I think."

"Yes," said Jack. "It's Saturday, but I meant the day of the month."

Howard shrugged again. "No, I don't know. Does it matter?"

Jack raised his eyebrows. "Oh, it matters all right. Tomorrow is May first."

"So?"

"May Day, you dunce. Tomorrow is May Day. Buck says Birchport has a big May Day Festival. He says the whole village turns out and has a merry time. He once won a pie-eating contest there, and he plans to try again tomorrow." Howard looked back at the lean helmsman. He did not look as if he could win a pie-eating contest.

"Won't we have to work at something around the boat?" It did not seem reasonable to Howard that he would be given an entire day off.

"No," Jack said, and punched his brother's arm. "It's a free day."

"Are we to stay in the barn, then?" Howard asked.

Jack frowned slightly. "Well, you and Bert will. I am to be put up at O'Grady's Inn with the rest of the crew."

"Don't fret over me not going to the inn. I don't like O'Grady. Besides, if I'm at the barn, I can see the girls. I want to show them the book."

"Show them? Don't you mean give it to them?" Jack moved closer to Howard. "That is all you can do. You do know that, don't you?"

"I suppose so." Howard did not look at Jack.

"Forget the book," said Jack. "Let's talk about the festival. We'll have a high old time. Buck says there are all sort of competitions with money prizes: races, catching greased pigs, mule pulls, and—hear this—a sling contest."

"You're bound to win some prizes," said Howard, and he looked down at the hard earthen path beneath his feet to hold back a sigh. He would rather, he thought, walk the towpath than spend a day being beaten by Jack in one event after another.

Jack nodded. "And an idea just came to me. Why not ask old Cyrus if the girls can come with us?"

"Oh no." Howard put his hand out to catch at his brother's arm as if to stop him. "He would never let them go."

Jack smiled. "You're thinking of the old Cyrus," he said. "Not the Cyrus who wants me to court his grand-daughter."

A tightness grew around Howard's heart, and he thought he might have trouble breathing. So Jack knew, had known all along, and he did not object to the idea. "She's only fourteen," said Howard.

Jack just laughed. "But back to May Day. Cyrus might not let Sarah go, but I bet he will let Laura and Gracie."

"I won't go off with them without Sarah," Howard said. "I'd sooner not go myself than leave her behind."

"Why?" Jack looked closely at Howard. "Don't tell me you're sweet on the girl or something?"

"Don't talk like a fool." Howard shook his head. Then he shrugged his shoulders. "I understand how she feels, that's all." He did not add what he thought. She's like me.

Jack slapped at his brother's shoulder. "Then maybe I'll tell Cyrus we won't take any of them if he says Sarah can't go. I expect I can persuade him."

Howard and Bert were settled for the night in the

barn when Jack came with the news. Sitting with their
backs against the front wall of the barn, they were eating
the supper of chicken, fruit, and bread that Howard had
packed in Della's kitchen.

Jack was full of pride at having gotten Cyrus to agree
that Sarah could go. "I gave him my word that I will
keep my eye on her. I told him no one would laugh at
her. He said he trusts me to look after her. It will be a
real frolic for them."

Howard wondered how Jack would look after Sarah
and still enter all the contests, but he said nothing. It
would be he, Howard, who would see that no harm
came to Sarah, and he would find a way to talk to Laura
about the book. The thought made his heart glad.

"I'm off to the inn now," said Jack, and Howard
walked to the barn door with him. Jack pushed open
the door, and he laughed. "I'll give your regards to
O'Grady."

"Go drown in the canal," said Howard, and he was
about to close the door when Jack stepped back inside.

"Wait," he said, "that reminds me. I forgot to tell you
the best part about tomorrow. There's going to be a
daredevil show. A fellow called Amazing Alex. He's
strung up a tightrope near the Main Street Bridge. He's
walking across the canal, right at ten o'clock. Cyrus told
me about it, says there's lots of talk as to whether or not
the fellow will make it. They've got two platforms built
for him with a wire stretched between them. Cyrus said
even he might go watch." He laughed again, and this
time he left.

Molly, at work somewhere on the canal or asleep
in one of the changing-station barns, was not in her
stall, but Howard bedded down there, anyway. Warmer

weather made it unnecessary for him to burrow under the straw, but the spring night was cool enough to make him glad for his blanket. He wrapped himself in it and closed his eyes, but sleep did not come easily to him. He was filled with thoughts about the May Day Festival. He would, he decided, not enter any contests. It would be more fun to watch Jack. Ordinarily Jack would insist. "Don't be a spoilsport," he would say, and Howard knew he would not have been able to put Jack off except for Sarah. He would need to protect Sarah. He smiled to himself. Protecting Sarah would bring him considerably more satisfaction than entering the competitions.

# 10

# GOD, HELP MY BROTHER

Howard carved the words, and he whispered the words to himself over and over as a prayer. They were strange words, words he had never imagined he would be saying.

He awoke that morning with no idea of what lay ahead. He used his foot to nudge Bert until he opened his eyes. "Get up, you lug-a-bed! This is May Day!"

For breakfast they ate apples saved from their food parcel, and they had not finished when Jack appeared. "You're wearing your crewman's jacket," said Howard. "Aren't you afraid you will get grease or pie on it?"

Jack smiled. "I expect one of the girls will hold it for me while we are in the contests."

Howard drew in his breath. Might as well get it over with. "I won't be competing," he said. "Someone will need to be with Sarah."

Jack looked at him for a long time, then he nodded.

"You won't find the likes of me playing nursemaid to some girl when there is pie to eat and money to win," said Bert, and he threw his apple core at Howard.

Laura came to the door when Jack knocked. She wore a hat and looked quite grown-up. Gracie, her braids flying behind her, pushed around Laura and ran down the steps. "Let's go," she shouted. "May Day might be over before we find it."

Howard reached out to pat her head. "There's no rush," he said. "The festival lasts all day."

Laura turned back into the house to get Sarah, who appeared in a hat like Laura's. Her expression looked confused. "She doesn't know where we are going," said Laura. "I had nothing to point to, nothing to make her understand."

Howard watched Sarah's eyes. Her gaze darted first to Jack, then to Howard, and finally to Bert. She stepped back toward the house. She's afraid because she doesn't know Bert, Howard thought. Maybe it is wrong to take her to a big gathering, but he still wanted to. He believed Sarah would understand the events when she saw them, and he believed she would enjoy them. He stepped up to the door, and he put out his hand to Sarah.

Sarah's eyes searched Howard's face. Then she put her hand in his, and together they walked down the steps. Birchport was alive with people. On the town square, three boys chased after a pig. "Let's give that pig a real chase," said Bert.

Jack shook his head. "Let's look around some first." He moved away, and everyone followed except Sarah. She stood watching the pig chase, her head cocked to one side. She understands this, thought Howard. He wanted to tell her about the prize, so he made the money sign, putting out his hand, running his thumb over his fingers as if feeling money.

"Sarah wants to see this race," he called to the others, and they turned back. They watched as one boy caught the pig, but it slipped away and ran. Finally the smallest boy grabbed the pig, and held him. The man in charge came over to the boy, who let the pig go. The man took a half-dollar from his pocket, held it up for the crowd to see, and gave it to the boy. Howard made the money sign again. The crowd applauded. Sarah smiled and clapped her hands together. Then she, too, made the money sign.

"What are you doing?" Laura asked.

"I've got a book . . ." Howard said, but Jack pulled at Laura's arm.

"Come on," he said.

"I'll tell you later," Howard managed to say before anyone moved.

"Let's go to the other side of the courthouse," said Bert. "I heard someone say the pie-eating contest is going on over there."

"Good," said Jack. "I want to see Buck."

When they rounded the corner of the building, they saw a long table filled with pies. Four men sat at a smaller table. Whole pies set in front of them. Their heads were bent over the pies, and they shoveled pie into their mouths with good-sized spoons.

"There's Buck," Jack told Laura, and he pointed to the man at the end of the table. Three empty pie plates were stacked in front of him, and he worked on his fourth pie.

Howard counted the pie plates in front of the other men. "That first man is ahead of Buck," he said, "but just by half a pie."

Buck spooned in pie and swallowed it quickly. He had a big Adam's apple in his neck, and Howard watched the knot move up and down at an amazing speed. For a time, though, Buck could not close the gap between him and the big man who led. Finally, Howard noticed that the big man's pace seemed to slow slightly.

Jack noticed, too. "Watch," he whispered to the group. "He's slowing down. Buck will catch him." Finally, the big man put down his spoon, clapped his hand over his mouth, and ran.

"He's going to vomit," yelled Gracie. "Let's go watch." She started to move, but Laura grabbed her hand.

"Gracie," Laura said, "don't you dare take a step to watch someone be sick at his stomach." Gracie frowned and turned back.

They stayed and cheered when Buck was declared the winner. When he was given the prize coin, Howard again made the money sign. Sarah nodded her head and did the same.

Next, they moved on to the sling contest. "Come one, come all users of the mighty sling," called the man in charge.

"I'm getting in on this one," Jack said, and he stepped forward. Two others already stood ready to try the sling.

"Anyone else?" called the man. "Anyone else want to try his hand?"

"Why don't you try, Howard?" said Laura, but he shook his head.

No one else stepped forward. "You will shoot in order of volunteering," said the announcer. He pointed to each contestant. "One, two, three."

Howard noticed Jack pull himself up to stand tall, but the young man beside him was still taller. Both of them watched as a short middle-aged man took the loaded sling and walked a few steps, twirling it above his head.

A target had been drawn on a large piece of board that stood on a stand a few feet away. The crowd grew quiet as the man walked. Then the rock was flying through the air. It struck the circle, but not close to the bull's-eye.

"Good show!" called the announcer. The man seemed pleased with his achievement, but Howard shook his head. "Jack can beat that by a wide berth," he told his friends.

While the tall young man got ready to shoot, Sarah made the money sign, and she looked at Howard with a questioning expression. "Yes," he said, nodding his head and rubbing his thumb across his fingers.

"What are you doing?" Laura asked.

"I've just told Sarah that the winner will get money." Howard smiled, more pleased with himself than he had ever been. "A lady on the boat gave me a book. It tells all about this sign language for deaf people."

Laura's eyes grew large. "You have such a book? You have it still?"

"Yes, at the barn in my haversack."

Laura clasped her hands and drew them up under her chin. "Oh, Howard, oh."

"We can teach Sarah." Howard bit at his lip. Why had he not said, "You can teach Sarah"? He worried that Laura could not read well enough. Besides, he had studied all those days. He wanted desperately to be in on the teaching. But how could he?

"When can I see the book?"

Bert moved closer to them. "The other fellow just missed," he said. "Jack's up now."

Howard turned his gaze to the contest. Jack was winding up. "He'll win for sure," Howard said, but his mind was not on the event, and he felt certain Laura's wasn't, either.

Jack's rock hit the bull's-eye, and the crowd cheered. Jack held up his half-dollar. Sarah made the money sign. Howard nodded, and Laura laughed out loud.

"Let's go spend this money on apple cider for us all," said Jack when he was back with the group and had been thoroughly congratulated.

"No time for cider right now," said Bert. "I just heard a fellow say Amazing Alex is getting ready to make his walk."

"We'd better hurry," said Jack. "I want to get a good spot so we can see." He turned to move, but Howard reached out to stop him.

"I might not watch," said Howard. "Laura, maybe we could go back to the barn and look at the book."

Laura smiled and seemed ready to go with Howard, but Jack took her hand. "Not watch Amazing Alex? That's ridiculous. Laura wants to see Alex, don't you, Laura?" Jack did not wait for an answer, and Laura let herself be led away.

With a sigh Howard followed. There was no use to go against Jack, not ever. The canal banks were already crowded when they reached them. Standing behind people, they twisted to look between bodies to see. Amazing Alex stood on one of his platforms. He wore a tight red uniform with shiny silver spangles sewn to it. A very small man, dressed all in black, stood beside

Alex. The little man held a funnel-shaped horn. Every few minutes he put the horn to his mouth and shouted through it, "See the Amazing Alex in a death-defying walk across the great Erie Canal."

"Let's go up on the bridge," said Jack. "We can see better."

Other people had the same idea, and the group had barely found a spot on the bridge before it became very crowded. They pressed shoulder to shoulder with a row of people behind them. A man shoved his head between Sarah and Howard. Sarah began to squirm, and her face twisted with discomfort.

"Sarah's pretty miserable here," Howard told the group. He tried to hold her hand, but she broke away and began to push through the crowd. "I'm going with her," Howard called, and he followed the girl off the bridge.

On the canal bank, Sarah pointed toward home. Howard shook his head. Now he did want to see if Amazing Alex could really walk that wire. He took Sarah's hand and led her to a spot not far from the base of the bridge. Some people had the front row, but Howard and Sarah stood behind them. "We can at least see the top of his head here," he said, though he knew she could not hear him.

Howard kept his eyes on the space where he would see the performer's head, but he was aware that Sarah was looking back toward the bridge. He did not want her to miss seeing the walker. Reaching out to her, he put one hand on each side of her head in an effort to change the direction of her gaze.

Sarah would not be budged. Howard gave up, but

Sarah pulled on his arm. She began to make strange, agitated sounds, and she pointed toward the bridge. Gracie sat on the bridge rail. Howard could see that Jack had his arms tightly around the girl's waist. Howard knew the sign for safe. With his fingers closed, he crossed his hands in front of his body, then swung them free and faced them out. Sarah, of course, did not understand. He would have to think of a way to show her safe and then make the sign.

Just then, though, Gracie wiggled back, and Jack helped her off the rail to stand in front of him. Howard smiled and expected to see Sarah grow calm. She didn't. The sounds grew worse, and her face was full of terror. She reached for Howard's arm and began to move, pulling him after her. He did not resist her.

When they were near the base of the bridge, she stopped. This time it was Sarah who reached for Howard's head. She turned his face, then pointed under the bridge. Her high, frantic moans frightened Howard, and suddenly he understood them!

The wooden supports beneath the bridge swayed drastically. Any minute the bridge would fall! "Jack! Jack!" Howard called to his brother, but Jack's face was turned toward Laura, talking. Motioning for Sarah to stay, Howard ran for the bridge.

Alex began his journey on the wire, but Howard paid no attention. "Get off this bridge," he called as he pushed his way through the crowd. "This bridge is going to fall." No one seemed to pay him any mind. Finally, he was beside Laura. "Get off the bridge," he shouted. "It's about to fall. The braces are giving way."

Bert began to push through the crowd to get off. Laura and Gracie started to move, too, but Jack reached for Laura's arm. "It's all right," he said. "I've seen the braces on these bridges sway plenty. They're built to sway, but they won't fall."

"No, Jack, listen. This is different. Come and look."

"Alex is about to do his walk." Jack pointed in the direction of the performer. "I don't want to miss this."

"Laura," Howard pleaded, "please come with me."

Laura turned to look at Jack again, and Howard saw Jack shake his head.

Howard's heart beat frantically. He hesitated just a second, then he reached out for Gracie's arm. "You're coming," he said in the firmest voice he had ever used in his life. Gracie followed. Howard pulled her through the crowd. "This bridge is falling," he repeated over and over. Most people ignored him, but three or four moved with him.

"We'll go back out front," he told Gracie. "I'll shout up at them some more. Maybe they will believe me."

Back on the bank, Sarah, her face white, waited for them. Gracie went to Sarah, and they held on to each other while Howard shouted. "Come off the bridge." He waved his arms and called as loudly as he could, "Get off the bridge."

He saw Laura and Jack looking down at him. He thought he saw Laura start to move, but it was too late.

The sound of splintering wood and horrified screams filled the air. Bodies and boards fell together into the waiting water. Howard sprang from the bank, moving through the water, his eyes searching. Others, too, were looking. He saw heads appear as people righted themselves in the water. "Jack!" he called. "Laura!"

Someone clung to the bank in front of him, and Howard recognized Mac, his shirt torn and his shoulder bleeding, struggling to climb out. Without a word, Howard bent, took Mac's legs, and lifted, but he did not wait to see him scramble up.

Then he saw Laura. She stood in the water. Her hat was gone, and her fair hair fell in wet tangles "Are you all right?" he shouted to her.

"Yes," she called.

Howard was beside her now, and reached out to touch her shoulder. "Where's Jack?" She shook her head.

"I'll help you out," he said, but she shook her head again.

"No, I can manage. You find Jack."

Howard pushed on among the floating boards. Others searched, too, and Howard saw bodies being lifted from beneath the water. What if Jack was down there under the water? Then he saw him. Ahead of him a few yards, two men carried Jack between them, and they were lifting him to the bank.

Howard grabbed the bank and struggled to climb out. "Is he alive?" he called as he moved, but the men did not seem to hear him. A man on the bank pulled Howard up to a spot on the towpath. Howard, breathing too hard to speak, dropped beside his brother.

"He's breathing," said the man who was bent over him, "but he won't wake up."

"Jack! Jack! It's me. Open your eyes, Jack. Open your eyes, please." A large gash covered most of Jack's forehead, and blood ran from it. Howard tore off his wet shirt and pressed it against the wound.

"The doctor will be by directly," said the man who had helped pull him out. "I want to make sure everyone's been hauled out."

"Thank you," said Howard, but he did not look up. He pressed the shirt again to Jack's forehead. "Jack," he said, "can you hear me? Wake up, Jack."

Laura came then, with Gracie and Sarah. They knelt on the path beside Jack and Howard. "Where's the doctor?" Laura asked, and Howard pointed to where Doctor Pruett worked over a woman a few feet away.

Gracie and Sarah were crying. "We have to pray," said Laura. "We've got to ask God to spare Jack."

"Pray while you run home for blankets," said Howard, "He's awful cold."

Laura and Gracie went for the blankets. Sarah stayed beside Jack, her big blue eyes full of fear.

The girls came back with old Cyrus and blankets just as Doctor Pruett arrived. "Yes, cover him," said the doctor. He listened to Jack's heart, held his wrist to take his pulse, and examined his injury. Howard waited, barely breathing.

Finally, the doctor looked up. "The boy has a brain injury." He shook his head. "There's nothing to be done for him now. Take him home, put him to bed, and keep him warm."

Cyrus asked the question Howard couldn't. "Will he come around?"

"There's no way to tell. He could wake up right away. He could wake up much later." He sighed. "And, of course, he could slip away without ever opening his eyes."

"He won't," Howard said softly. "Jack won't give up. He won't."

"Are you his brother?" the doctor asked, and Howard nodded. "I thought so," said the doctor. "I see the family resemblance, same facial structure."

Howard looked up, amazed. No one had ever said he looked like Jack. "Thank you, sir," he said.

The doctor stood, took his bag, and started to move away. "There will be a wagon along soon," he said. "They will take him home."

Home, thought Howard, is far away. If Jack died, how would he ever tell their mother? How could he ever be the bearer of such news?

"Begging your pardon, Doctor Pruett," Cyrus called, and the doctor turned back. "I be wondering did anyone die here today?"

"Four," said the doctor. "Four so far," and he hurried away with his bag before Cyrus could ask their names.

When the men with the wagon came, they loaded Jack with his blankets into the back. Howard climbed up to sit beside him. The girls would walk home, and Cyrus rode up front with the men. "We'll put him in my bed," he said, turning to Howard when they had begun to move. "I'll sleep in the pantry."

Howard held on to Jack's hand and listened to the clop of the horses' hooves on the road.

Mistress Donaldson met them at the door. "Is he dead, then?" she questioned as the men unloaded the blanket-covered form from the wagon.

"No," Howard called. "He is not dead, and he will not die!" He jumped from the wagon and ran to the door. Live, Jack, he repeated over and over in his mind. Live. You're obliged to live.

Mistress Donaldson folded back the covers on Cyrus's bed, and the men placed Jack there, dropping the blankets that had covered him. She took off his shoes, and Howard pulled off Jack's wet britches and shirt before she spread blankets over him. Next she went for a pan and a cloth to wash his face.

Howard looked around for a chair, but there was nothing in the little room except a bed and a small chest. He went to the kitchen for a chair, put it as close as possible to the bed, and settled himself there.

"I suspect you're hungry, lad," Mistress Donaldson said to Howard when she had finished washing Jack's face and tying a white cloth bandage around his head. "There's beans and bread aplenty in the kitchen."

Howard shook his head. "Thank you, no," he said. "I'll just wait here until Jack wakes up. I can eat then."

Mistress Donaldson made a sad clucking noise with her tongue, wiped at her eyes with her apron, and left the room.

Laura and Grace, when they arrived, came in to stand silently at the end of Jack's bed. Laura's dress had almost dried now, but her thick hair was still wet and tangled. Her face was as white as the bandage on Jack's head. "I'd rather they had put him in the pantry," said Laura softly. "Our da died in this bed."

Howard kept his eyes on the gentle rise and fall of the blankets with Jack's breath. "Our father died, too." He bit at his lip. "My father and Jack's, but he was older, and weak with consumption. Jack is strong," he said, his voice rising. "No one is stronger than Jack. Jack will not die!" A tingle went through his body, a sensation of strength, and he stared at his brother, willing the strength of his own body to pass into Jack's. "Live, Jack," he said, this time aloud. He did not notice when the girls tiptoed from the room.

Howard sat beside his brother and watched the shadows in the room grow longer. Captain Wall, Buck, and Bert came to stand about in the room, talking softly to each other. Captain Wall put his hand on Howard's shoulder. "I'll hire temporary help," he said. "Your jobs will be waiting for you, yours and Jack's, when he's able." The boy looked up at the man and nodded. No words would come to his lips.

Just before dark, Cyrus came in with a lamp. "Go have a bite, laddie," he said. "I'll stay by your brother. It won't change things, you being away from the bed. What will happen will happen. Jack, now he be in the hands of God."

Howard let Cyrus pull him up from his chair, and he wandered into the kitchen. The girls sat at the table with their mother. Mistress Donaldson stood as Howard came in. "I'll fix you a plate, my lad," she said, but he shook his head.

"I couldn't eat." He put his hand on his stomach. "Nothing would stay down. Mayhap I'll walk a bit to clear my head."

Laura came to him with a hunk of bread and a slice of salted pork. "Take this," she said. "You've need of food to stay strong for Jack."

He nodded his head, took the food, and went out the door. At first he moved without direction, eating, and letting his feet take him where they would, along the canal and past the shops. At the fallen bridge, he stood for a long time, looking and wondering.

Finally he moved on. After a time, he stopped and looked around him. He was, he realized, near the boys' school. He looked across the street at the big white building. Lights came from every window, and Howard imagined boys studied in those rooms. Once, such a thought would have filled him with envy. Now, his insides were frozen with fear for Jack.

He stood for a while and looked at the building, then crossed the street. Without knowing exactly why, he wanted to talk to the teacher.

He went to the high front steps. A few days ago it would have been impossible for Howard to climb the tall steps and knock on the big front door. In his long-ago life before this morning, he would have been too shy, but now he climbed easily and knocked without hesitation. "I need to see Mister Parrish," he said to the boy who answered.

The boy, who seemed to be about his own age, opened the door, looked at him, and raised his eyebrow. Howard felt the boy stare at his dirty, disheveled clothing. "Who are you?" he asked.

"Tell him it's Howard Gardner," he said without dropping his gaze. "Tell him it's the boy from the snow."

Almost at once, Howard heard footsteps on the wooden hallway floor, and Thomas Parrish appeared. "Howard," he said, and he came to shake the boy's hand. "Are you all right?"

Howard rubbed his hand across his eyes. "The bridge that fell . . ." He stopped. He could not talk about Jack, not now. If he talked about Jack to this kind man, he would cry. Howard did not want to cry, but if he had not come to tell Mister Parrish about Jack, why had he come? He looked about the wide entry hall. Bookshelves lined the wall. There must be books everywhere in this building, he thought.

Howard knew Mister Parrish looked to him to say

more. He swallowed, waiting, then began to speak. "I wanted to tell you that I'm not going back to the canal," he said. The words seemed to burst from him, unplanned. "I'll have to work, but if there's a way, I'd like to study here."

Mister Parrish used his hand to usher Howard through the hall. "Come to my office," he said. "You look as if you need a chair."

Howard began to speak even before they were inside the room. "I'm staying because of my friend," he said. "Cyrus's granddaughter, she's a deaf-mute." He took the chair Mister Parrish indicated without a break in his explanation. "I have another book, and it's about talking with your hands."

Thomas Parrish sat behind his desk, and when Howard stopped talking, he nodded. "Sign language," he said. "It's taught in schools for the deaf. There's a wonderful new one down in the city of New York."

"Sarah can't go away to school. There's no money. Besides, her grandfather would never allow it. I can teach her, though. I've already started." Howard rubbed his thumb across his fingertips. "Sarah knows that's the sign for money."

"Very good," said the man. He leaned toward Howard. "You look as if you've been through something today," he said. "Were you on the bridge that fell?"

For a second Howard felt confused, then his head cleared. "My brother was," he said. "Jack. He was hurt bad." He stood suddenly. "I've got to go back there. I've been gone too long. Jack might . . ." He turned to the door.

Thomas Parrish walked from behind his desk. "Let me get my rig. I'll drive you back."

Howard stood and shook his head. "Thank you, no," he said. "It's kind and all, but I believe I can walk there while you're getting your horse. It isn't far, sir."

"All right," said the teacher. He walked with Howard to the door. "You come back later, Howard," he added after they had said good-bye. "I think I can arrange for you to go to school here."

"I'll have to work," Howard said again, and he moved through the door. "I send money to my mother."

"You could study here part-time," said the man.

Howard turned back from the second step. "Thank you, sir," he said. "I will come back when . . ." He stopped. "I will come back, no matter what happens."

"Good. I'll say a prayer for your brother tonight, Howard," he called as the boy went down the steps.

"Yes," said Howard without turning around, "you do that, please. You say a prayer for Jack Gardner. You tell God that Jack should live to be a captain on the Erie Canal."

The May evening was cool, and Howard shivered as he walked. He thought of Della. She would be proud of me, Howard thought. I made up my mind, just like she made up hers not to stay on her island and work in the fields. Tomorrow he would tell Laura that he was staying in Birchport.

When he reached the house, he knocked at the door. Gracie came to let him in. "Is there any change?" he asked her.

She shook her head. "No, Grandpa is in there now, but he would have called out if Jack woke up or died." The little girl clapped her hand over her mouth, then went on. "I shouldn't have said that. I should have said naught a word about dying."

Howard reached out to touch her cheek. "It's no matter," he said. "Saying a word doesn't make it happen, Gracie." He stepped back. "I'm going to the barn to get something. I'll be right back."

Being in the barn seemed strange. The door made the same loud creak as he opened it. The stalls were the same. The same four mules stood in the last stalls. The straw was the same. How could everything look the same, smell the same as it had in the morning? How could everything be the same when the world had changed so completely?

In Molly's empty stall Howard dug beneath the straw for his haversack. He wanted to take it with him to Cyrus's house so that he could add to his carving. Then he took his blanket, stuck it under his arm with his bag, and walked to the barn door. Just before he left the barn, he looked back. There had been a boy who lived in this place for the winter, but that boy was gone. He had changed into someone else.

When the others had gone to bed, Howard sat with his board. The lamplight was enough to see Jack's breaths as they lifted the covers slightly. For a long time Howard watched. His body ached with exhaustion, and his eyes closed over and over. He would, he decided, spread his blanket beside Jack's bed. He would sleep there for a time, waking often to put his hand on Jack's chest.

First, though, there was a thing he had to do. He took his knife from his pocket, picked up his board, and carved his prayer for Jack. Then he sat for a long time with the board pressed to his chest.

# 11

## WE ARE SILENT NO MORE

Howard looked at his writings. There were ten now. He felt good about carving his history in the board. His words would last. The only thing better would have been to carve his words in stone, like the ones part of the canal had been cut through.

That first night after Jack's fall, Howard slept hard. Just before sunrise, he woke with a start. He had not checked on Jack for quite some time. Afraid of what he might find, he lay for a moment, listening, but no sound came from his brother's bed. He pushed back his blanket, got to his knees to see the bed. Jack's chest moved up and down with breath. Relief spread through Howard's body, giving him the strength to move.

With a cloth he had dipped into a bowl of clean water, he touched Jack's dry lips. "Wake up, brother," he said. "It's a new day, and we're needed on the canal."

Jack moved his head on the pillow, but he did not open his eyes. Howard bit at his lip. He would have to write a letter to Ma. He would ask Laura to get the quill pen, ink, and paper he had given her, and he would write the letter. Tomorrow he would post it. Ma had to be told. She would be surprised, Howard thought, to learn that Jack had been injured. He looked down at his brother. "Ma would have expected such from me," he said, "but not from you."

Gracie came to call Howard to breakfast. "Ma says you're to come to the table and put some real food in your stomach."

Howard left the door to the bedroom open. "I need to be listening for Jack, in case he wakes up."

"I'll help you listen," Gracie promised, and she left the room.

Howard took the brown book from his haversack. He held it close to his body and slipped it, unnoticed by the others, into his lap when he sat down.

While the girls and their mother put food on the table, Howard waited, saying nothing until he had filled his stomach with potatoes and eggs. He took a big drink of tea, drew in his breath, and started. "I saw a deaf girl on the canal," he said. "Her mother and grand-mother talked to her with their hands, making signs, and she talked back."

Mistress Donaldson gasped. Cyrus put his tea mug down without taking a drink, and Laura reached across to grab at the hand Howard had left on the table. "Tell them about the book," she said.

"There's a book! The lady gave it to me. I want to use it to teach Sarah."

"You think you could learn Sarah how to talk with her hands?" asked Mistress Donaldson, and there were tears in her eyes.

Howard nodded. "I can teach, and Sarah can learn."

Suddenly Cyrus pushed back his chair and stood up. "Whoa, the lot of you!" he said. "This is my house, and I won't have you coming in here to get Sarie all stirred

up. Laura's one thing, but not Sarie. I won't have it, I
say!" He reached out to Howard, took his arm, and
pulled him up. "Get up, you young troublemaker, you.
Get up and get out of my house."

Howard did stand, but he made no move to leave.
"Begging your pardon, sir," he said. "I know this is your
house, and I am grateful for your generosity to my
brother and me, but you do not own Sarah." He motioned toward her. "She is a person, sir, and she deserves
a chance to speak, if not with her mouth, then with her
hands. We all need to tell what comes up from inside
us." He paused for a second, drew in a deep breath, and
went on. "Yesterday, sir, it was Sarah, out of all the people gathered round, who knew that bridge was going to
fall. It was Sarah who made me see how the braces were
about to give way. If not for Sarah, Gracie would have
been on the bridge, too, and she might be dead or injured like Jack. Look at her now!" He waved his hand
toward Sarah, who sat looking from one face to the
other. "She wants to know what's going on right now.
Give her a chance, sir. She is a person. Give her a
chance."

Cyrus sat back down in his chair, almost, it seemed to
Howard, drawn into a ball. He had never noticed before
how small a man Cyrus was, and he looked even older,
old and frightened. "I don't believe in this hand-talking
business." He shook his head. "Sarie ain't right, and I
won't have her troubled by a lot of nonsense."

An idea came to Howard. "Let me show you," he
said. He put his hand into his pocket, took out the
purse he carried with him always, and removed a pre-
cious half-dollar. Pushing back his plate, he cleared a
space on the table. He put the coin on the cleared

spot, then laid a fork and the book in line with it. Next, he went to Sarah, who sat on the other side of the table. Pulling on her hand, he led her to the three items.

The room was silent. Howard passed his hand over the three items, then turning to Sarah, he used his thumb to rub across his fingertips. "It's the sign for money," he said to the others, and again he held his hand up to make the sign for Sarah.

The girl nodded, picked up the coin, handed it to Howard, and smiled. Laura and Gracie clapped. Mistress Donaldson burst into sobs. Only Cyrus remained quiet, and he leaned his face into his hands. Howard led Sarah back to her seat. He stood by the table. For a time no one said anything. Then Mistress Donaldson spoke. "Set yourself down, Howard Gardner, you're going nowhere." Then she turned to her father. "Howard will teach Sarah, Da," she said. "Howard will teach Sarah, and God be praised that he is willing."

Laura left her chair and went to her grandfather. "It will be all right, Grandpa," she said, touching his shoulder. "Don't be afraid."

Cyrus raised his head and turned to Howard. "She's like a cup, like a fine china cup, Sarie is. She'll break, too, terrible easy."

Howard nodded. His body felt shaky. "I know, sir," he said. "I promise I'll be careful." He turned from the table then. "I need to see about my brother."

After he had closed the door, he carved the message. Sarah was learning to speak, and he was learning to speak out. His body still shook, but inside he felt good.

All morning Howard stayed quietly beside his brother. He did not think about how he would manage to stay in Birchport to teach Sarah. He thought only about Jack and would not leave him when the noon meal was ready. "We'll fix you a plate, then," said Laura, who had come to call him, but it was Sarah who carried the food to him.

He nodded his thanks to her, took the plate, and sat down on his chair beside the bed. Sarah moved quietly to the other side of the bed, where she stood looking down at Jack. Howard realized then that she had not been in the room before. She pressed her hands to each side of her face, and tears rolled down her cheeks.

Howard wanted to go to comfort her, to remind her how her warning had saved several people from falling, but of course he couldn't. Someday he would be able to say such things to her. "Today is an important day for you, Sarah," he said as she studied Jack's face. He took the brown book, touched her shoulder, and held it out to her.

Sarah took the book and opened it, studying the words and diagrams. Reaching out first to touch her hand, Howard made the sign for learn, taking knowledge from a book. He placed his open, down-turned fingers of his right hand on the book. Then he closed his fingers, raised them, and placed them on her forehead.

Sarah's blue eyes searched his face, questioning. Howard pointed to himself, then to Sarah, then to the book. He made the sign for learn again. Next he turned the book to the word *money*, showed her the diagram, and made the sign with his fingers and thumb. He pulled the half-dollar from his pocket.

A smile began to grow in Sarah's eyes and spread beautifully to her lips. She took the book and pressed it to her heart.

"We're starting, Sarah," Howard said. "We've got a long way to go, but we're starting."

After the meal Howard felt suddenly very tired. He spread his blanket again on the floor and drifted at once into sleep.

When he woke, Laura sat beside Jack. "He seems different," she said. "Restless, like."

Howard looked down at his brother. It was true. Jack no longer lay quietly. Lips moving and eyebrows jerking, he did not look peaceful at all. Howard washed his face. "What's wrong, Jack?" he said softly. "Are you dreaming, falling again from the bridge?" He brushed the thick, dark hair back from the bandaged forehead. "You're all right. Just open your eyes and you'll see. You're safe in bed. Old Cyrus put you right in his own bed. Isn't that something?"

All the rest of the day Howard sat beside Jack's bed. Laura and Gracie came and went, their voices quiet and their eyes down. When the evening meal was ready, Laura came to stand beside Howard. "You go now," she said. "I'll stay with Jack."

Howard shook his head. "I'm not hungry," he said. "I'm still full from before," but she brought him two hunks of hot buttered bread on a plate. "Thank you," he said, and he forced himself to eat.

When the bread was gone, he put the plate on the chest and went to stand by the window. Outside, a spring twilight slipped across the yard and the hill. The soft light filled him with a sudden loneliness. If Jack died, Howard would feel so alone. He wiped at a tear that rolled down his cheek, then went back to Jack.

"Want to hear something that will make you wake up and tease me?" he said. "I was about to cry just now, about to bawl like a baby because I was afraid you might die. That was silly, wasn't it?"

He reached for Jack's hand. His fingers closed around Jack's, and he jumped, startled! Jack had squeezed his hand. "Jack," he said, his voice rising. "You heard me, didn't you? Do it again, Jack. Squeeze my fingers again so I'll know you can hear me."

Laura came in just then. "What is it?" she asked, hurrying to the bed. "Did something happen?"

Howard nodded his head quickly. "He squeezed my hand. I was talking to him, and he squeezed my hand."

"I'll get Ma," said Laura.

Howard kept Jack's hand tight in his. Mistress Donaldson came rushing into the room with Laura. The woman went to the bedside and moved Howard away. Leaning over Jack, she lifted an eyelid and peered into this eye, let it drop, and lifted the other. Then she stood quietly, studying Jack's face.

When Howard could stand the silence no longer, he reached out to pull at her dress sleeve. "He squeezed my hand! Did Laura tell you? He squeezed my hand!"

The woman nodded. "Aye, she told me." She did not look at Howard.

"Well, then," he said, bending his body in an effort to see her face, "what do you think?" He straightened and looked at Laura. "It's a good sign, isn't it?"

Mistress Donaldson sighed, and she turned to Howard. "I hope so, lad," she said softly. "By all that's sacred, I hope so!"

"But why wouldn't it be?" Something about the look in her eyes made Howard's voice shake. "Why wouldn't it be a good sign for him to squeeze my hand?"

The woman took her apron and wiped at her face.

"I'll not lie to you, lad," she said. "It ain't my nature to be false." She breathed heavily again, and Howard waited. "It could be a good sign, him squeezing your hand." She pursed her lips. "Was it to happen again, I be inclined to think it more likely, but, lad, there's a thing some call the quickening, like when life comes into a babe."

Howard shook his head. "I don't understand."

"Well, they say that sometimes before a person dies, he might quicken, have a burst of life. I've seen it happen. My Jacob, the girls' father, he done it. Hadn't been able to talk or set up a bit, but just before he died, he set up, he did, and he asked for his pipe."

Howard stepped around the woman. "That's not what's happening," he said, and he bit hard at his lip. "That's not it at all. Jack is not going to die." He dropped his head and closed his eyes tight. "I couldn't bear it if he did. I just plain could not bear it."

He felt a hand touch his arm and opened his eyes to see Mistress Donaldson beside him. "You could bear it, lad. You'd have to. There ain't no choice about such. You'd go back to that towpath, and you'd walk behind them mules same as always. You'd be different inside, awful different, but you'd still walk the towpath."

The evening took a long time becoming night, but finally Howard could not see the birch tree outside the window. Jack continued to toss about on the bed, and Howard waited. When the family went to bed, he spread his blanket on the floor, rolled himself in it, and after a long time, he slept.

Sometime in the night he woke. Someone had called his name! He was certain of it. He stayed still, listening. "Howard." He threw back his blanket and sprang to his feet.

"Jack!" he shouted. "Jack!"

"Could you get me a drink of water?" Jack said.

Howard took the cup from the chest, helped Jack raise up, and held the cup to his lips. "That's good," Jack said. Then he looked around. "Where are we?"

"This is old Cyrus's bed," said Howard. "You've been unconscious. The bridge, do you remember?"

"Oh," said Jack, "Oh, yeah. The bridge fell. Is Laura all right?"

"Yes, Laura's all right, but four people died."

"You told me it was going to fall," said Jack. "I should have listened to you."

Howard closed his eyes and slowly shook his head. "You should have done just that. It's a thousand wonders you're still alive," he said, and he smiled.

# 12

# JACK WAS A SIGHT TO SEE

It was the first really lighthearted carving for Howard, and he smiled as he carved. It happened the night after Doctor Pruett's morning visit to examine Jack. "He appears to be making a full recovery," the doctor said, and he closed his black bag. "I would suggest at least two more days of bed rest."

Howard walked out with the doctor and paid him with the half-dollar from his own pocket. "You've come to this house enough unpaid," he said.

The doctor climbed onto his carriage. "I suppose it's back to the canal for you two brothers as soon as possible," he said.

"Jack will make a great rush of it, I'm sure, but as for me, I'm not going back. I mean to find work here in Birchport." Howard slipped his hand into his pocket to touch the purse. He still had six dollars, enough to eat on for a time while he looked for work.

Thinking, he walked slowly back up the steps. Inside the house, no one knew that he did not intend to return to the canal. He had stated his intention to teach Sarah, but he had not come right out and said he was not going back to the boat. When he did, it was certain that Cyrus would not let him sleep in the barn. Nor did it seem likely that the man would take him in. Cyrus was not that sold on Sarah's learning.

Then, of course, there was Jack, who would rant that Howard belonged back on *The Blue Bird*. Howard closed the gate slowly behind him. Two days—the doctor had said Jack should rest at least two more days. He would say nothing until he had to.

Gracie sat on the porch, her feet crossed under her. In the lap of her dress was a small bag with walnut meat spilling out of it. "Eating nuts, are you?" Howard asked her.

Gracie shook her head. "These are old. Ma overlooked them too long in the pantry, and they don't taste good now, but I been coming here every day." She pointed to the birch tree. "There's a squirrel up there. I've named him George Washington after the man in your book."

"The first president, the father of our country," Howard said. "Your squirrel should be proud of so noble a name."

"Yes, him. Well, when you go inside, I'll put a piece of walnut on the porch for George Washington to get. I do it every day. Then I stay all quiet, and he comes to get it. First I started with the ground below the tree, but now he'll come right up the steps. Pretty soon I'll get him to come inside."

Howard laughed. "A squirrel's a wild animal, Gracie. He won't come into a house with people in there. Besides, if he did, your ma would have him in a stew in a wink."

"Cook the father of our country," said Gracie, "that would be terrible ornery. Mayhap I'll ask George Washington to come in at night."

Howard shook his head. "Don't try to touch the thing. He'll bite and scratch something furious." He went on into the house.

Jack, propped on pillows, frowned at Howard when he came in. "Two more days in this bed. *The Blue Bird* will be almost to Buffalo by that time. How are we going to catch up to her? Maybe we could catch a hurry-up boat. They go fast."

Howard shook his head. The hurry-up boats were the only ones on the canal allowed to go as fast as possible. The boats rushed to repair damage in the earthen bank because such a break threatened canal travel. "Hurry-up boats won't take passengers. You know that. If they did, they'd never get their work done. The men on those hurry-up boats aren't going to change the rules just for us."

"It could be almost two weeks before *The Blue Bird* is back in Birchport. What are we going to do all that time?"

"I don't know about you, but I'm going to teach Sarah sign language and maybe do some reading lessons with Laura." Howard went to the chair to pick up the brown book. "In fact," he said, "I'm going to see about starting with Sarah right now. You should try to go back to sleep."

"I've been sleeping two days," said Jack. "You'd best spend all your time on Sarah. You don't have time to teach Laura, too. You only have a week or two."

Howard sighed. The blow to his head had not changed Jack. Everything was still a contest with him. Jack, who thought Howard belonged on the canal with him, would also not like Howard's being around Laura so much. Say right now that you're not going back, Howard told himself, but he went quietly from the room.

Most of the day Howard worked with Sarah. Mistress Donaldson, glad to excuse the girl from her chores, bustled about her work with a smile on her face. Laura and Gracie worked in the kitchen garden during the morning. Before the noon meal, Mistress Donaldson brought up potatoes from the root cellar. "'Tis a good thing we've more growing in the garden now," she said, and she laid them on the table to peel.

"Potato," said Howard, making sure Sarah saw his lips move. "Potato." He took a potato in his hand. Then he made the sign, the down-turned right index and middle fingers thrust repeatedly onto the left fist.

Cyrus was not as pleased as his daughter. When he came in to eat, he looked suspiciously as Howard and Sarah made signs to each other over their food. "Don't make no sense to me," he muttered.

"You can learn to do this, too," Howard said.

Cyrus grunted. Then he turned to Laura. "Pass me more potatoes," he said.

"No," said Howard. "Let Sarah do it." He reached across the table, touched Sarah's hand, then pointed to Cyrus. "Potatoes," he said, and made the sign. Sarah picked up the bowl that sat between her and Laura. She handed it to her grandfather.

"I don't know as I believe in this," Cyrus grumbled, but Howard had caught a look of pleasure in his eyes.

In the afternoon he had a chance to work with Laura. They sat at the table just as before, but Laura read much better now. "I practice every day," she told him.

"You need the second primer," Howard said. "I'll buy it for you."

"I'd not like to see you spend your money," said Laura.

Howard smiled. "I'll see about borrowing one from Mr. Parrish at his school," he said, and happiness spread through him. It felt good to be sitting at the table again beside Laura, his hands at times brushing against hers on the book. Sarah no longer stood at a distance with a look of longing. She moved about the kitchen, doing chores and practicing the signs for the things there.

They closed the book, and Howard wrote the sentence "The girl can read her book" for Laura to read. After the third sentence, Laura stopped and sighed. "I've something to tell you," she said, but she did not look at him.

Something in her voice made Howard steel himself for bad news. "Grandpa came to me in the garden. He said Jack had a word with him this morning."

"Oh," said Howard. He could no longer sit still beside her. He got up and moved to stand by the kitchen window.

Laura paused for a minute, then went on. "Jack wants to keep company with me, he does."

"Oh," said Howard again. He jammed his hands into his pockets. "What did Cyrus say?"

"Grandpa said yes. He's pleased as can be."

"That's good, I guess," said Howard, and his shoulders sagged.

"Well," said Laura, "I said no. I told Grandpa I don't be ready to be courted by anyone." She twisted her body toward him. "Would you look at me please, Howard Gardner?"

Howard turned. "Yes," he said.

"I told Grandpa to pass on to Jack that he could ask

again next year. I didn't tell Grandpa, because, of course, he'd rave, but what I really want is to go to school."

"I know. It's what I want, too."

"I think we are cut from something of the same pattern, Howard," she said.

He smiled and came back to the table. "I'll write more sentences," he said. All the rest of the day Howard thought about what Laura had said, ". . . cut from something of the same pattern." Laura understood him. Did that mean she understood that he, too, would someday like to keep company with her? He wondered if he would ever be able to say so. He could not quite imagine saying those words aloud. Besides, there was Cyrus. Laura's grandfather already had her future husband picked out.

That night Howard spread his blanket again on the floor beside Jack's bed. "We'll go back to the barn tomorrow night," he said.

"I don't know as Cyrus will hear of that," said Jack. "He is pleased to have us as guests, I believe."

"We can't stay here eating the man's food for two weeks." Howard took off his shoes, but accustomed to sleeping in his clothes, he did not undress. He stretched himself out on the blanket. "I mean to find work tomorrow."

"Work? For two weeks? I doubt anyone would take you on for that short a time."

Howard drew in a deep breath. "I may not go back to the canal," he said. "I may find work and stay here in Birchport."

Jack laughed. "You tried that, remember? No, your place is on the canal with me." Jack seemed to think the subject was closed, and Howard said nothing more.

When the lantern was blown out, though, he did not sleep. He lay on the floor going over the day's events in his mind.

From the other side of the house came the sound of Cyrus's snoring. Howard had heard the sound before, and he imagined that it was very much like the sound an elephant might make. Another sound came to his ears. He pushed himself up to rest on his elbow. The sound came again, but it was faint, overpowered by the snoring. He listened for a moment, but he heard nothing more and lay back on his blanket.

He had just drifted off to sleep when a scream from Mistress Donaldson woke him. "A ghost!" she yelled. "There's a blooming ghost in here!"

Howard jumped up, ran through the main room, and into the bedroom where Mistress Donaldson and the girls slept. Mistress Donaldson stood on the bed she shared with Gracie. Her head, covered with a white cap, almost touched the low ceiling. Laura and Sarah were also awake, Sarah sitting up and Laura standing beside their bed. Only Gracie, her face turned into her pillow, seemed to sleep through the noise.

"Saints preserve us!" screamed the woman. "He's flying again!" There was no shade on the window, and bright moonlight poured into the room. Howard followed the woman's pointing finger, and he, too, saw it across the room. A white shape seemed to float from the chest to the washstand. "I seen him first when he come into the room," yelled Mistress Donaldson. "On the floor he was, but then he took to flying."

Howard moved toward the form. "Be careful, Howard," Laura called. Howard stepped into the room and was at the end of the bed when he heard Gracie's giggle, stifled by the pillow.

"Out of the way, brother," said Jack. Howard turned to see his brother behind him. Jack had armed himself with the walking stick Cyrus kept by the door. He had not yet changed from his winter underwear. He stood in the doorway wearing his long johns, the stick raised above his head, ready to strike.

Howard almost laughed, but he did not step out of his brother's path. Instead, he moved closer to the form.

Mistress Donaldson saw Jack then. She got out of the bed and went to him. "I don't know, lad, as you should strike it," she said, her voice worried. "It just come to me that it might be the ghost of my poor Jacob, come back to see how we're getting on."

Howard could see the form better now. "I doubt it is anybody's ghost," he said. He was close to the form now, and it moved from the washstand back to the chest. White strings drifted after it. Howard reached out to grab one of the strings and lifted the white cover.

"A squirrel!" yelled Laura. The animal scurried down from the chest and ran toward the doorway. Howard got to the bedroom door in time to see the squirrel run into the main room and out a crack in the front door.

He handed the white cloth to Mistress Donaldson. "My apron," she said. "I put it on a chair in the kitchen." She turned the apron over. "I left a bit of cake in the pocket. The creature must have got his head in the pocket and couldn't shake the thing."

"I'm going back to bed," said Jack. He put down the

walking stick and moved quickly across the main room to disappear into Cyrus's room.

"It's a mercy Da didn't wake up," said Mistress Donaldson. "The man can sleep through any ruckus, he can. He'd have been considerable excited, and ranting about who left the door open."

Laura laughed. "You were considerable excited yourself, Ma, and Jack in his unders!" She laughed again. "I wish Gracie had been awake, though. She'd have had herself a merry time. Mayhap I'll wake her now and give her a good laugh."

"No," said her mother. "I don't want her stirred up now. You can tell her tomorrow."

"Good night, all," said Howard, and smiling, he went back to his blanket.

Jack lay on his bed. His eyes were closed, and he breathed as if asleep. Howard, certain his brother could hear him, said, "You were real brave, brother, ready to fight that squirrel. Looked good, too, in your long johns." He chuckled, and he went to light a candle. He laughed again when the words were carved.

The next morning Gracie sat outside the bedroom door, waiting for Howard. "You won't tell about George Washington, will you?"

He shook his head. "Nobody has asked if I have an opinion as to how that squirrel got in."

She laughed. "Did you ever see such carrying on? I just got me a peek once or twice, but you got to see it all."

He smiled. "It was fun, but you'd better not let George in again, Gracie."

"I won't. I was plumb amazed that he come in at all. Then when he stuck his head in Ma's apron, I made a streak to get into bed because I knew he might rouse someone up."

The conversation at breakfast was all about the squirrel. Gracie's only comment was, "I wish I could've seen it all."

Cyrus reached for the biscuits. "Who left the door open, so the creature could get in? That's what I'd like to know." He turned to Howard. "Did you go out after I went to bed?"

Howard opened his mouth, but Gracie spoke first. "Mayhap it was me, Grandfather. I recollect going out to get a look at the moon. I'm real interested in the moon right now." Gracie looked down at her plate.

Cyrus put butter on his bread. "Mind what you're doing, lassie," he said. "We don't want wild creatures roaming around in our cottage."

"Lands, yes," said Mistress Donaldson. "We're likely to have a mule in my apron next time." She chuckled.

"A mule would be fun," said Gracie.

"This is absolutely my last day in this bed," said Jack when Howard went to pick up his dishes after breakfast. "I need to be up and about."

"I'm sure Cyrus will be glad of having his bed back. We'll sleep in the barn tomorrow night."

"Oh, I don't know as that's a fact. Cyrus will take his bed back, but I wager he'll not have us going back to the barn. Want to stake a half-dollar against mine that we'll spend the next fortnight in the pantry?"

"We've no money for gambling," said Howard. "Cyrus will want payment if we eat here that long. He's not running a home for wayward boys."

"I doubt he'd see his future grandson-in-law as a wayward boy," said Jack, and he laughed.

Howard turned away to keep Jack from seeing his frown. "I'll take these dishes. Then I'm going to town," he said, and he offered no explanation.

He went first to see the Main Street Bridge. He had drawn the bridge for Sarah and had taught her the sign for fall, the down-turned index and middle fingers of the right hand placed in the upturned left palm, the right fingers flipped over, coming to rest palm up in the left hand. Howard had watched as Sarah made the sign over and over. A tear had rolled down one cheek. She had looked at Howard. He had made the sign with her, and he had nodded his head. They had sat for a time without doing other signs.

Now Howard watched men work on the bridge. The old structure had been torn down, and a new frame was being built. Howard stood watching for a while. The memory of seeing Amazing Alex on the wire flashed through his mind. He saw the man in the red suit with the silver spangles, saw him start his walk across the wire, but that vision was quickly replaced with pictures of the people on the bridge, people Howard had tried to warn. He remembered Laura's face and Jack's. He remembered the shattering boards and the falling bodies, but he did not remember what had become of Amazing Alex. Had the man made it across the canal?

Alex's walk had caused the falling of the bridge. The falling was big in Howard's life, so big that he could not even form words in his mind to say how big. He had to know about Alex. He had to know now. He moved as close as he could to the workers. One man stood on the bank. He took a board from a stack and held it out to a man on the bridge frame.

"I say," Howard called to the man as he walked toward

him. "Can you tell me, did Amazing Alex walk across the wire the other day, or did he fall? I didn't see."

The man turned to look at him. "He made it across," he said, "but no one noticed much. The bridge fell, you know, a terrible sight. It's lucky you are not to have been here. They say Amazing Alex was so upset that he canceled the crossing up at Little Falls." The man turned away with his board.

Howard moved on down the narrow street. On his right, boats filled the canal, almost end to end, with barely enough room to pass each other. The May sun shone bright on the packet boats and the passengers who filled the upper-cabin deck, ladies with dresses and parasols of vivid colors, men in business suits and top hats, and laughing children.

On a lineboat, a man sat on top of a huge wooden keg with a monkey in his lap. The man shouted, "Good day to you, lad," and the monkey tipped his red hat. A man staggered from one of the taverns and tried to jump onto a packet boat. He missed and fell into the canal. The bowman threw the man a rope and pulled him aboard.

With one look back over his shoulder, Howard turned onto a side street, walking away from the canal and toward the boys' school.

# 13

# SARAH HAS CHANGED

Howard carved the words at night by the light of a candle in a tiny little room that had become his new home.

Jack had been right about Cyrus. "Go back to the barn? That's balderdash, and I'll hear none of it," Cyrus said the first morning Jack was out of bed and eating breakfast with the family. Cyrus shook his head and reached for his pipe. "It's the pantry for you, Jack, my boy." He paused and looked at Howard. "Oh, and your brother be welcome, too, if you consider the feather bed big enough for two."

Jack shot a triumphant smile across the breakfast table at Howard. "Thank you, sir," said Howard. "I won't be here long. I'm going to find a job as soon . . ."

Jack interrupted. "We'll both be back on *The Blue Bird* in two weeks or less."

Howard changed the subject. "Well," he said, "I want to spend as much time as I can with the girls. Sarah and Laura are making real progress learning the signs." He turned to look at Laura. "And I've borrowed the second primer for your reading lesson."

"Maybe I'll help you," said Jack.

Howard looked at his brother for a second before he spoke. "Jack," he said, "we have a pattern, you know, a regular way of doing the lessons. I don't know as there would be a way for you to help."

"You can help me, Jack," said Gracie. "I'm working on learning to track animals. I'm thinking maybe I'll be a bear tracker when I am all grown up."

Jack smiled weakly. "Maybe I'll do that, Gracie," he said. "Maybe I'll learn to track bears, too."

When the breakfast things were cleared away, Howard and Laura got out the new book. "Mr. Parrish said we could keep it as long as we need it," said Howard.

Jack hung about the kitchen for a while. "I could take Laura outside and help her," he said once, "and you could work with Sarah in here."

Howard bit at his lip. Maybe he should listen to Jack's suggestion, but Laura shook her head. "Thank you, Jack," she said. "It's good and kind of you to want to help, but I'm used to Howard."

She smiled. "If he's not weary of me, I believe we'll just go on the way we are. I like to be in on Sarah's lessons, anyway, so I can learn to talk to her."

Jack shrugged his shoulders. "All right," he said. "I just thought I'd help. Maybe later we can all go to the canal and watch the boats."

"That would be nice," said Laura, and Jack left the room.

"I wanted to tell you about going to the school," said Howard when they were alone. "Mr. Parrish says I can take classes come fall." His voice rose with emotion. "Mathematics and science in the morning or literature and history in the afternoon."

"Oh, Howard," she said. "My heart is glad for you. It is!"

"Thank you, Laura. Mr. Parrish says there's no reason I can't be a teacher, like him. It would make me happy to be like Mr. Parrish." He stopped, suddenly embarrassed by the joy of it all and by Laura's desire to go to school, too. "And Laura," he said, "I believe we can find a way for you. If we think and are watchful, I believe we can find a way for you to go to school, too."

She smiled at him. "What will you do for money, Howard?" she asked.

"Well," he sighed. "There's the rub. I've got to find a job, and a place to stay." He shook his head. "If I can't find a job, it's back to the canal for me."

"I don't suppose Grandfather's likely to let you stay in the barn."

"No, not likely. I'm not Jack."

"He'd let Jack stay with us," she said, and they laughed.

"There's one job that's open," he said, "but I've no chance of securing it."

"Why? What job is it?"

"At O'Grady's Inn. I saw the sign when I went past his place yesterday. He hired me once, but yelled at me when another hoggee told him I had English blood. O'Grady's Irish, and he hates all the English." Howard frowned. "There's no hope he would hire me."

"That's not right," said Laura. "He lives in America now. Grandpa was born in Ireland, but he doesn't dislike you because you have English blood."

"No," said Howard, and he smiled. "He dislikes me because I'm not Jack."

"You should talk to O'Grady. Just stand up to him, and tell him he is not being fair."

Jack shook his head. "Oh, no, there's no reasoning with O'Grady."

"You stood up to Grandfather, I mean about Sarah. You stood right up and told him he didn't own her. You were very brave, Howard."

Pleasure washed over him like cool water against his skin on a hot day. Still, there was no denying the truth. "I couldn't stand up to O'Grady. He'd likely knock me down and step on me." He shuddered. "No, there must be another way. Oh, but do you want to see how he misspelled the words on his sign? I think you could do better, no more schooling than you've had."

Howard took up his pencil and wrote the words of O'Grady's sign. "*Kithon Boe Neded.*" Laura pulled the paper to be directly in front of her, and she studied the words.

"They're all misspelled," he said. "Can you spell them correctly?"

"*Kitchen* should have a *c* in it," she said, and she spelled aloud. "K-i-t-c-h-o-n. Is that right?"

"Almost," he said, taking his pencil to cross out the *o* and make an *e*. "What about *boy*?"

"That one's easy, b-o-y, and *needed* should have a double *d*, I think."

"You got *boy*, but *needed* has double *ee*'s after the *n*."

"Well," said Laura. "If O'Grady won't have you as kitchen help, mayhap you can teach him to spell. You're right smart of a teacher, Howard Gardner. You're just that good!"

Howard thought he might burst. Laura thought him brave and smart. Laura had turned down Jack's offer to help her. She preferred him to his brother, at least when it came to teaching. It was enough for now. "Let's have a go at this new book," he told her. You'd look a fool with a foolish smile the whole time, he told himself, and he fought to keep the corners of his mouth from turning up.

They were not quite finished with Sarah's lesson when Jack came back in and sat down at the table across from them. "Let's go down to the canal now," he said. "I want to tell the girls about my job as a bowman."

From habit, Howard almost closed the brown book, but he stopped himself. "In a minute," he said to Jack. "I want to tell Sarah first what we're going to do. She knows the sign for *see* already." Howard put the fingertips of the first two fingers on his right hand just under his eyes. Then he swung his hand straight out.

Sarah made the same sign, and she nodded her head. "We'll see the boats," he told her. He turned the pages of the brown book. "Here," he said, and he pointed to the sign for boat. He cupped both hands together like the hull of a boat and moved them forward in a bobbing motion.

Sarah looked confused, and shook her head. Howard picked up his pencil and drew a boat like the packet boats Sarah had seen on the canal. Then he made the boat sign again. This time she nodded her head. She turned to Laura and made the sign for *see*, followed by the sign for *boat*.

"See boats." Laura said. "Yes, we'll see the boats."

Jack took Laura's hand and pulled her toward the door. Howard followed with Sarah and Gracie. They walked through the town, stopping sometimes to watch one boat or another. Sarah pulled at Howard's shirtsleeve and made the sign for *fall*.

"Wait," he called to Jack and Laura. "Sarah wants to go down to see the bridge."

Jack turned back to his brother. "It's not a sight I fancy seeing. Besides," he said, "we don't have too long. I want to get on down to the docks. Tell her you'll take her later."

Howard looked at Sarah, who made the sign again. There had been so few times in her life that she had been able to ask directly for something. "You go on down to the docks with Laura and Gracie. You can tell them all about your job. I'll take Sarah to see the bridge, and then we'll join you."

"All right, then," said Jack, "we'll meet you on dock three." He turned with the girls toward the docks while Howard and Sarah headed toward the Main Street Bridge.

At the bridge, they stood watching the workers. Sarah put her open hands, palms facing her eyes and fingers slightly curved, beneath her eyes and moved them down toward her mouth, her head dropped slightly. "Yes, sad," said Howard, nodding his head. He too made the sign. They watched for a few minutes more while Howard thought about that day. It was sad, of course. People had died, and he remembered the terrible fear he had felt for his brother. Yet, standing there beside Sarah, he knew that without the falling of the bridge, without his being right about something so important and Jack's being wrong, without that triumph he would never have had the courage to stand up to Cyrus about Sarah and the signs. Without that day he would not be planning now to break away from the canal, where Jack's future lay, to find his own spot.

A great lightness came to him. He would go now to join Jack beside the canal, but he would find a way to avoid going back to work there. He made a beckoning sign to Sarah, and they headed for the docks.

They were on the first dock when suddenly the monkey with his little red hat ran between the legs of two ladies in front of them. The women screamed. The monkey grabbed Howard by the legs, jumped up into his arms, and hid his face against Howard's neck. "It's all right," Howard said to people who had crowded around him. "He won't hurt anyone. He belongs to a man on that lineboat." He pointed to the same boat he had seen yesterday, still fastened to the dock. "I'll return him."

Most of the people moved on. The monkey lifted his face to look at Sarah. Then he tipped his hat to her. She laughed and clapped her hands. "Let's take him back to his owner," Howard said, and he pointed again to the boat, but he noticed then that it had drifted slightly away from the bank. He wasn't sure Sarah could jump that far, and he could not help her and hold the monkey. "You stay here," he said to her, and he made the sign for *stay*.

He was gone only the few minutes it took for him to find the monkey's owner, who was asleep on the opposite side of the cabin. He woke the man, gave him the monkey, and went back to make the jump to the dock. He heard the sound of laughter even before he came around the cabin of the lineboat. Sarah stood on the dock. Four boys pressed around her. One of them held Sarah's wrist. Another of them reached out to touch her hair. "Hey," said one of the boys, "you reckon she can't talk?" He leaned close to Sarah's face. "What's wrong, girlie, cat got your tongue?" His face was turned away from Howard, but the voice was familiar. Mac! Mac O'Hern reached out his hand to touch Sarah's cheek.

A great rage came up from inside Howard, and he shouted, "Let her be! Let her go, and get away from her, all of you!" In an instant he made the jump, landing only a few feet from the boys. "Let her be!" he yelled again, and he ran at the boy who held Sarah's wrist.

"Says who?" the boy demanded, but he turned Sarah loose, spinning to meet Howard with fists up. The first blow made him stagger back, but he did not fall. From the corner of his eye, he saw another boy with his fist tight and aiming for his stomach. Then he saw something that surprised him.

Mac reached out to grab at the boy's arm. "Ah, let him go," he said. "It wouldn't be no fun licking him, four against one. Besides, we ain't got time for a fight right now." He turned and started away. "Come on," he said.

His friends followed, one of them bumping hard into Howard, making him stagger back and almost lose his balance. When he regained his footing, he turned to Sarah. She was gone! Howard's mind raced. Had he seen her since making his run at the boys? He knew she had stepped back when her wrist had been released. Had she been there still when Mac made his speech about leaving? Howard could not remember. Fear began to grow inside him. He whirled in one direction, then the other. The docks were crowded, and he caught no sight of her fair hair.

"Sarah," he called, knowing she could not hear him. "Sarah, Sarah." Which way had she gone? He had no idea. If she ran into the boys who had bothered her earlier, or others like them, he would not be there to fight for her. He stood frozen for a moment, Cyrus's words running through his mind. "She's like a cup, like a fine china cup, Sarie is. She'll break too, terrible easy."

If Sarah got hurt, Cyrus would never let him teach her again. What if things turned out even worse? What if someone took Sarah? Someone might take her onto one of the boats. Sarah might never be seen again. A cold sweat broke across his forehead.

If she went toward dock three, there was a good chance Jack or one of the girls would see her. Howard ran then in the opposite direction from the docks, pushing his way through groups of people who moved about on the streets.

He moved fast, but still he searched the streets, looking quickly over the crowd and into each corner. Somewhere Sarah was terrified. Somewhere Sarah was crying. He had to find her.

A stout woman with a large basket on her arm stood watching the passersby from the doorway of a tavern. Howard was almost past her before he could bring his body to a stop, but he reached out and grabbed at the signpost to slow himself. "Excuse me, madam," he said, breathing hard. "Have you seen a girl go by? She's taller than I am. She's wearing a calico dress, her hair is fair and in braids?" The woman looked at him, a questioning expression on her face. "Please," he said. "I've got to find her."

"I did," said the woman, "and I wondered, her crying the way she was."

"Oh." Howard felt his heart leap. "How long ago was it you saw her?"

"Well," said the woman, "it was just after we opened this morning. I'm sure of that."

"Not the one I'm looking for," he called over his shoulder as he ran on.

He passed a tannery, where a man stood in front of the shop scraping a skin. At the door of two taverns, he paused long enough to look into each of them, imagining what bad things could happen to a helpless girl like Sarah if she came into a room of intoxicated men.

He had gone almost through the length of the town in one direction and was about to turn back when he caught sight of her on the steps of a church. A man stood with his back to Howard, and he had his hand on Sarah's shoulder. Howard drew in his breath, ready to make a run at the man's back, but just then he saw the collar. The man was a priest.

Howard let out his breath and moved toward Sarah and the man. Sarah did not see him. She was busy making a sign for the man. Her left hand, thumb side up, rested in her right hand. The left hand was pushed up slightly by the right. *Help.* Sarah had been taken a few times to church by her mother, and she had run there asking for help. Howard had imagined that she had run away in fear, but now he knew she had gone for help.

Smiling, he moved toward her. When she saw him, Sarah smiled, too, and reached out to touch his arm. "She's deaf, Father," he said to the priest.

"I know, my boy." The priest frowned. "She kept making a sign to me, but I could not understand. I've heard of the sign language, but I've never learned it."

Howard reached for Sarah's hand. "She was asking

for help," he said. "She thought some boys were about to gang up on me, and she was asking for help."

"Well," said the priest, "I'm sorry I couldn't understand, but you look as if you didn't fare too badly."

"I'm all right. At least I am now that I've found Sarah." He started to move away but turned back to say a thank-you to the priest.

"Come back to see me, lad," said the man. "I'd like to learn more about talking with your hands."

"I will," called Howard, and with Sarah beside him he hurried on to the third dock to meet Jack and the girls.

The three were sitting on kegs near a loading boat when Howard and Sarah found them. Jack jumped up when he saw them. "Where have you been?" he asked. "We were getting worried."

Gracie shook her head. "Jack was worried," she said. "Laura said you would take care of Sarah. She said you wouldn't let nothing happen to her."

Howard smiled. "Sarah's getting pretty good at taking care of herself," he said. "One of these days, she might not need any of us so much."

"If we don't hurry," said Jack, "you'll be needing some good help yourself, explaining to Cyrus why the girls weren't back in time to help get the noon meal."

They moved back through the town. Up ahead, Howard saw O'Grady's sign, KITHON BOE NEDED. What would happen, he wondered, if he did as Laura had suggested? O'Grady couldn't kill him for asking again for a job. At least he didn't think O'Grady could do that. He slowed his steps and looked into the window. Mistress O'Grady was in the front. She stood beside her husband, near the counter.

Jack and the girls were ahead of him. Jack turned back. "Come on," he said. "You can walk faster than that."

"You go on," Howard said, and he stopped in front of the inn. "I'll come along later."

"You're not going in there!" Jack leaned his head toward the inn. "Why would you do a fool thing like that?"

Howard swallowed hard before he spoke. "You all go on," he said again. "There's something I've got to do."

"You are going in there," Jack said. He stopped and put his hands on his hips. "Howard Gardner, you must be daft."

Laura smiled at Howard, and she pulled at Jack's arm. "Let Howard do what he wants to do," she said, and she began to walk on.

"If you go in there," Jack said, "I'll not be hanging around to help you out."

Howard said nothing. He waved at Jack, turned toward the door, and put out his hand to open it. Just before he went in, he looked again in Jack's direction. He was moving along with the girls, but he shook his head as he walked.

Inside the inn, Howard took a deep breath. Then he walked to where O'Grady leaned against the counter, which his wife wiped with a cloth. Mistress O'Grady stopped cleaning to look up at Howard and smile.

Howard moved on and stopped beside the man. "I've come to ask about the job," he said.

O'Grady turned to Howard, and his eyes searched the boy's face. "I've seen you, boy. Where is it I know you from?"

Howard squared his shoulders before he spoke. "I

came in last winter," he said. He kept his eyes on
O'Grady's as he spoke. "You told me I could have the
job, but then Mac came along. I guess he told you I was
English. You wouldn't have me then."

"Well," said O'Grady, "is it true? Are you a bloody
Englishman?"

"My father's people were from England, but they
came to this country before my father was born." He
crossed his arms in front of his chest. "What difference
does it make, anyway? We're all Americans now, sir, and
I need a job. I'd work hard."

"Cheeky little bugger, aren't you?" said O'Grady.

"I need a job, sir," Howard repeated.

"Why not give the lad a chance?" said Mistress
O'Grady.

The man looked at the woman, then back at Howard.
For what seemed a very long time he said nothing, only
scratched at his dark beard. Then he took a step toward
Howard, who forced himself to stand still.

"I'll give you a go at it," he said. "But it ain't a full-
day job. That be why Mac quit us to go back to the
canal. Our daughter's come home, left her no-good
husband. She helps some in the kitchen, but her mother
here thinks we can't push her too hard. You'd work just
after the noon rush and on to closing. All day on Saturday and Sunday. Pay's five dollars a month."

"Could I sleep in the kitchen?"

The man nodded his head. "There's a little closet
you can have, and you eat what's left at the end of the
day. We'd want you out of the way, though, until you
come in to wash dishes after the noon rush."

"I have someplace to go," said Howard. "I plan to go
to school." He was surprised to see O'Grady smile.

"I believe in schooling," he said. "Went to school my-self, I did. That's why I could write up the sign." He pointed through the window.

"May I bring the sign in for you, sir?" said Howard. O'Grady nodded, and Howard went out to get it.

"Put it behind the counter," O'Grady told him. "I save it. No need making a new one every time a new boy's required."

"You won't be needing it for a long time," Howard said, but he put the sign on the shelf behind the counter.

"Come in tomorrow by one," said O'Grady, "and don't be late. I won't stand for lateness."

"Can I sleep here tonight?" Howard asked just be-fore he opened the door to leave.

"You can," said O'Grady, "but I won't be giving you breakfast. You eat only after you work, and be back here before we close at eight. I'll not be waiting around for the likes of you before I go upstairs to bed."

"Thank you, sir," said Howard. He closed the door behind him, and then he broke into a run. Down the crowded street he dashed, feeling so light that he thought it might almost be possible to fly. He consid-ered going to the school to tell Mr. Parrish the news, but he turned instead away from the village and toward Cyrus's house.

When he was near, he slowed his pace. He would go inside. Everyone would probably still be at the table. Should he make his announcement right away, or should he wait and tell Jack when they were alone? By the time he reached the house, his mind was made up. He would keep the news and tell Jack first.

The kitchen door was open, and he paused in the doorway. Mistress Donaldson was at the stove, dishing up food. "Come in, Howard, boy," she said. "We're just about to eat, we are."

Laura was near the table, ready to sit down. She looked up at Howard, a question in her eyes. He nodded his head at her, and then before he could stop himself, it came pouring out. "I'm not going back to the canal," he said. "I have a job at O'Grady's Inn."

"Wonderful," Laura shouted. "I am—"

Howard, afraid Jack would get in a word, interrupted her. "The best part is I don't go to work until one, at least during the weekdays. I'll be able to go to school two hours in the mornings when the new term starts and come here to teach you and Sarah."

"It's a lunatic idea," said Jack. "You've tried it before." He began to shake his head, but Howard turned away.

"I'll not be looking the other way and letting you sleep in the barn," said Cyrus.

"I am sleeping at O'Grady's, starting tonight."

"If you only work supper, that's the only meal O'Grady will give you," said Jack. He shook his head again.

"I lived on less most of last winter," he said, and he crossed his arms.

"You'll not go hungry," said Mistress Donaldson, and she pulled back a chair for him. "Not while you're teaching my girls. You've done a fine thing for these lassies, you have, Howard Gardner. It was a gift from God, it was, when you come to our door on Christmas Day." Howard sat down, and the woman put her hand on his shoulder. "It's hope I have that you'll teach Gracie, too, someday." She laughed. "Mayhap even my own self. Now fill your plate."

## 14

# I AM A HOGGEE NO MORE

During the rest of the spring and all summer, Howard divided his mornings between teaching at Cyrus's house and reading in an empty schoolroom. "You could take the books with you," Thomas Parrish told him, "and save yourself the walk over here."

Howard shook his head and traced his finger around the inkwell on the desk where he sat. "If it's all the same to you, sir," he said, "I like coming here. I like sitting in a schoolroom, even if it's empty."

Often Mr. Parrish would come into the room where Howard read to discuss the books. "I know how the creature suffered," Howard told him about Mary Shelley's *Frankenstein*. "I felt almost that out of place on the canal."

Thomas Parrish smiled. "You're here now, Howard," he said, "where you belong. You'll advance in your studies quickly, I'd say. We might have you teaching the younger boys some by next year and studying full-time."

Sometimes Howard remembered the day he stood outside of the girls' school and pitifully tried to hear what was read inside. Now he himself could go into a school. Now he had come home. He never wanted to work on the canal again, and yet he found himself drawn to it. Almost every evening after O'Grady's closed, he would walk along the banks. Finding a quiet spot, he would sit on the bank so close to the passing boats that he could almost touch them.

He would look long and hard at the boys who drove the mules past him. He missed the mules, especially Molly, and he hoped some hoggee would put flowers on her harness.

That summer the boys all seemed young to Howard, and he knew how their feet ached. He did not wish to ever live far from the canal. He did not wish to forget the boy he had been there. He would always remember that he had been a hoggee and that the winter had not killed him.

Working for O'Grady was not easy. Sometimes Howard would come in to find his employer in a terrible temper. The first several times O'Grady threw frying pans or pieces of firewood at him, Howard felt lucky to have ducked in time not to be hit. After a time, he realized the man was not actually trying to hit him.

Cyrus still grumbled about how book learning would do Laura no good, but he could not hide his pleasure in Sarah's signing. "You can learn to talk back to her," Howard told him. Cyrus shook his head, but Howard noticed he stayed sometimes, standing about the kitchen, watching.

Laura noticed, too. "I'd wager that Grandpa will be signing soon," she said one morning.

Howard stayed up with the travels of *The Blue Bird*. Whenever possible he would take the girls and be on the dock when the boat stopped. There would be a minute to speak to Jack. One day in late summer the boat needed a few hours for repairs, and Jack came unexpectedly to Cyrus's house. "Forget the lessons," he said when he appeared in the kitchen doorway. "We've a few hours for a holiday."

They went to a sweetshop that opened out to the canal, and Jack bought them apple dumplings. They sat at a round table to eat, and they watched the boats. Several times Howard felt his brother's eyes on him from across the table, but when Howard looked up, Jack only smiled. Finally, Howard could not be quiet. "What is it?" he asked. "You've been looking at me, no studying me is more like it."

Jack laughed. "All right," he said. "I'll admit it. I've been thinking you did right not to go back to the canal. I've been thinking you've grown, too. I guess school and all agree with you."

Howard nodded. "I have grown."

Jack reached across the small table to punch at Howard's arm. "But don't go thinking you're the biggest toad in this puddle," he said, and he laughed again. "I've got an idea or two of my own to work on."

Laura and Gracie pressed Jack to say more, but he shook his head. "Not now," he said. "We'll wait and see. It might be I'll be sending you a letter soon."

The letter, when it came, was addressed on the outside to Howard Gardner, O'Grady's Inn, Birchport, New York. Mistress O'Grady came carrying it to Howard. "It's a post for you," she said. "We never had a boy before that got a post."

Howard unfolded the single sheet and read.

*Dear Howard,*
*I know Laura wants to go to school, and she is not likely*
*to consider any suitor until she's had at least a taste of*
*education. I've made it my business to see that she gets to*
*go to school, and Sarah, too. I looked up your friend*
*Mrs. Brewer, in Schenectady. She is a lady of considerable*
*means, and she said she often wondered how you had*
*progressed with her book. I explained to her how pleased*
*we would be to see Sarah go to a school, and she has set*
*up a scholarship for her at the school in the city where her*
*granddaughter went. Laura is to go, too. She will stay*
*with Sarah and will be able to attend classes herself.*
*I know you are thinking Cyrus will never allow it,*
*but I am sure I can persuade him. Say nothing about it*
*to Cyrus until I come to talk with him. I suppose you*
*should go ahead and tell Laura what I have done for her*
*and Sarah so that she can be prepared. I will arrange*
*passage on* The Blue Bird *for them.*
*This is certainly a point in my favor, but I am sure*
*you will be happy for the girls.*

*As ever,*
*Your brother,*
*Jack*

Howard read the letter twice before he looked up at
Mistress O'Grady, who stood watching him. "Is it bad
news, then, lad?" she asked.

"No," he said. "It is good news, just a bit of a shock,
that's all." He looked again at Jack's "As ever." He
sighed, folded the letter carefully, and put it in his
pocket.

Laura was overjoyed when he told her. She jumped
up and began to move about the kitchen, laughing and

talking at the same time. After her excitement had
calmed a bit, she came back to the table to sit beside
Howard.

"But I'll miss you, Howard," she said, "and I doubt
I'll ever have a better teacher."

"You will," he said. "You will have fine teachers;
Sarah, too." He smiled, "Just think, Sarah can learn to
read." He dropped his eyes, took a deep breath, and continued. "After you've been to school, I won't be your
teacher anymore. I hope you might consider me for the
position of suitor."

"Oh." Laura pulled in her breath with surprise.
"Oh, Howard, I will. I will most certain consider you."
She reached out to touch his hand. "And I'll write you
letters," she said. "I'll write to you and tell you all about
our school."

"And the ocean. You can tell me about the ocean."

She clasped her hands under her chin. "Yes, the
ocean. Do you think, then, that Jack can really persuade
Grandpa?"

"I do," said Howard, "and your mother will help if
need be."

Jack needed no one's help. He arrived one week after the letter to speak privately with Cyrus, catching
him down at the barn. When he came back to the
house, he shouted at the door, "Pack a satchel, Laura,
and one for your sister. You're to leave on *The Blue
Bird* with me this very day." He came into the room,
put his hands on Laura's waist, picked her up, and
whirled her around.

Howard went with them to the boat. It felt strange
to him to be standing on the dock waving to the girls
on board. Jack came to Howard just before the mules

started to pull the boat. "Cyrus is sure I will marry Laura," he said.

"It might turn out that way," said Howard, "but if it does, it will be because Laura wants it, not because you beat me at some sort of contest. Laura is not a slingshot competition. It's a thousand wonders, but I am finished with competing. I am not in the contest. I will be your rival no more."

Jack looked at him. "Of course you'll compete," he said, and he smiled. "You always do." He reached out to punch Howard's shoulder. "I've got to jump quick," he said. "Good-bye, little brother." He ran to hop on.

Della stuck out her head from the kitchen window. "You done good, Howard," she called. "Della is proud of you."

That night in his closet room he carved for the last time on his board. Della was proud of him, and he felt proud of himself. Jack did not believe him, but his brother would eventually know the competition had ended.

Howard stacked his fourteen boards on the shelf above his blanket. He was glad he had recorded his story, but that chapter of his life was over. From now on, he would write with a pen in a journal. He was a student now. He took a history book from the shelf, and he began to read.

# AUTHOR'S NOTE

I was inspired to write about Sarah because my niece has a little girl who shares the same challenges as Sarah. Sarah's grandfather feared that she would be made fun of because of her inability to speak or hear, and his fears were realistic. In fact, Sarah would, at that time, very likely have been called deaf and dumb rather than deaf and mute. I did not use the word *dumb*, because I do not like it. *Dumb*, of course, means "unable to speak," but many people did treat deaf-mutes as if they were stupid or unable to think well. Sarah's life would have been much easier today.

Howard Gardner was not a real boy, but there were many real boys who worked on the Erie Canal as hoggees. The word is pronounced hoe-gee, and it comes from a similar old Scottish word used to refer to a lowly worker.

It took eight years to cut the Erie Canal through 363 miles of mountains, valleys, rivers, and swamps from the Hudson River to Lake Erie. During the construction, more than a thousand laborers died, many from malaria. The original canal was only forty feet wide and four feet deep, but when it was finished, three thousand canal boats traveled the waterway. Not much of that first canal remains to be seen today, but parts of the later canal have been refurbished to be used for recreational purposes.